The FLOODS

THE FLOODS

GOOD NEIGHBORS

BY

COLIN THOMPSON

ILLUSTRATED BY

CRAB SCRAMBLY

HarperCollins*Publishers*

The Floods #1: Good Neighbors
Text copyright © 2005 by Colin Thompson
Illustrations copyright © 2008 by Crab Scrambly

Library of Congress Cataloging-in-Publication Data
Thompson, Colin
Good neighbors / by Colin Thompson ; illustrated by Crab Scrambly.
— 1st American ed.
p.   cm. — (Floods ; #1)
Summary: A family of wizards and witches living in an ordinary
neighborhood in an ordinary town decides that they have had enough
of the noisy family living next door and makes them disappear.
ISBN 978-0-06-113196-7 (trade bdg.)
ISBN 978-0-06-113199-8 (lib. bdg)
[1. Witches—Fiction. 2. Wizards—Fiction. 3. Neighbors—Fiction. 4.
Magic—Fiction. 5. Humorous stories.] I. Scrambly, Crab, ill. II. Title.
PZ7.T371424Goo 2008   2007029613
[Fic]—dc22   CIP
                                                          AC
Typography by David Caplan
1 2 3 4 5 6 7 8 9 10
❖
First published by Random House Australia, 2005
First American edition, HarperCollins Publishers, Inc., 2008

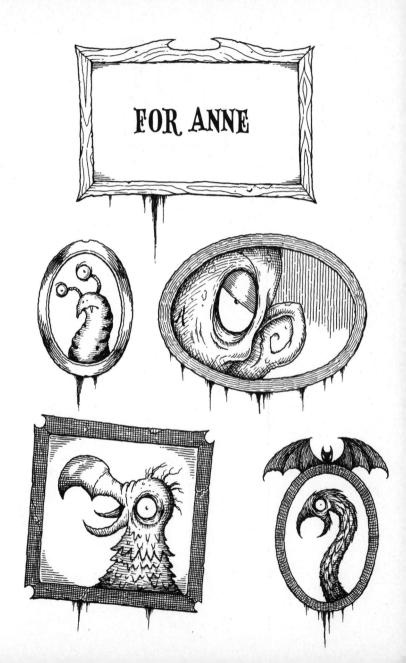

FOR ANNE

At first glance, as long as you are at least a
hundred feet away and see them from
the back on a dark autumn evening when it's
raining, the Floods look like any other family.
There is a mom and a dad and some children.
They all have two eyes, one head, two arms
and two legs, and hair on top of their heads—
except Satanella, who has no arms but four
legs and hair all over her body.

At second glance, especially if you're *less* than a hundred feet away and see them from the front, the Floods do not look like any other family. Mom and Dad and most of the children always wear black clothes. Even Satanella wears a black collar encrusted with black diamonds against her black fur. Only the youngest, Betty, is different. Her hair is

blond and she wears ordinary, brightly colored clothes and skips a lot.

The Floods are a family of witches and wizards—even Betty, although she looks almost normal. She likes looking different from the rest of them. It makes her feel special. It also lulls the world into a false sense of security. She is the only one of the Floods who people don't cross the road to avoid.

They even feel sorry for her and say, "Look at that sweet little girl having to live with those weird people, poor thing."

It all started when Betty's mother, Mordonna, decided that six children who were witches or wizards was enough. Valla, Satanella, Merlinmary, Winchflat, and the twins, Morbid and Silent, were each, in their own weird and scary way, the sort of children any witch or wizard parent would be very proud of.

Satanella, for example, is not the family pet. She's actually one of the children, but because of an unfortunate accident with a shrimp and a faulty wand, she was turned into a fox terrier. Although it's possible to reverse the spell, Satanella has actually grown to like being on all fours.

Merlinmary also has hair all over her body,[1] but she is not a dog, even though she does growl a lot and likes chasing sticks.

"I would like a little girl," Mordonna said to her husband, Nerlin, after the twins were born. "A pretty little girl who wants to dress dolls up

---

[1] *No one is sure if Merlinmary is a he or a she because he or she is so hairy that no one can get near enough to find out. Throughout this book Merlinmary will be referred to as "she," but please remember she might be he or something weird that isn't either.*

4

instead of turning them into frogs. I want a little girl who I can cook with and make cakes that taste like chocolate instead of bat's blood."

"But, sweetheart, we're wizards and witches," said Nerlin. "Turning things into frogs and blood is what we do. Our families have done it since the dawn of time."

"I know, and I adore frogs and blood," said Mordonna, "and I love our six wonderfully talented, evil children, who are as vile as your wildest dreams. I just want one pretty little girl to do ordinary mother-and-daughter things with."

"But you grow death cap mushrooms with the twins and you sharpen the cat's teeth with Valla."

"Yes, yes, I know," Mordonna replied, "and I love all those things, but what about knitting and painting pictures of flowers?"

"What's knitting?" asked Nerlin, but Mordonna had made up her mind. She was going to have one more child, and that child would be a normal, ordinary girl with no magical powers. And instead of being made in a laboratory using an ancient recipe book, a very big turbocharged wand, and a set of shiny saucepans, the way some of the other children had been, this new child would be made the same way as you and I were.[2]

When Betty was born, she looked just like the pretty little girl Mordonna had dreamed of. Of course, being a wizard's child, she was very advanced for her age, and by the time she

---

[2] *Well, I was. I can't say how you were made. You could have been knitted for all I know.*

was three she was helping her mom make soufflés and had knitted a cardigan for her granny, Queen Scratchrot. (The queen, with several other friends and relations, is buried in the backyard and feels the cold on winter nights because most of her skin has rotted away.)

But no matter how "normal" she looks, Betty still has magic inside her. It's mostly little things most people wouldn't notice, like when she reaches for a book way above her head and suddenly the book is there on the table. Or when a glass floats across the kitchen, fills itself up at the tap, the water turning into juice with two ice cubes and a straw, and then floats back into Betty's left hand. 잔 ∘ 일절 ∘ 지푸라기

Where the Floods live is a <u>bit like them.</u>[3]
From a distance it looks ordinary, but up close it isn't. They don't live in a big dark <u>menacing</u> castle in Transylvania Waters like all their other relations. They live in a normal

---

[3] *My editor asked me to name the town where the Floods live, but I won't, because you might feel safe and secure knowing they don't live near you—and we wouldn't want that, would we? And if you do live in their town, you might start bothering them and get yourself turned into a toad, and then your parents might sue me, unless being a toad is an improvement on what you are now.*

country in a normal city in an ordinary street in a house with a front yard and a backyard. Except the Floods' house is kind of different.

It isn't because the hedge tries to reach out and touch you when you walk by, and it isn't because the yard is barren. It isn't because there are three black clouds always hovering over it, even on a bright, sunny day, or that there are no leaves on the trees. And it certainly isn't because the Floods are nasty to everyone. They aren't. If people weren't too scared to ask, the Floods would happily lend them their lawn mower (if they had one) or give them a cup of sugar.

When the Floods bought the house, it was the same as all the others on the street. It had a neat lawn in the front and back with beds of pretty flowers. The front door was red, and

10

the windows had bright white <u>frames</u> and shiny clean glass.

The only thing the Floods didn't change was the front door.

"A lovely <u>shade</u> of fresh blood," Mordonna had said, "but the rest will have to go."

They painted the window frames black and added <u>cobwebs</u> and dead flies. They <u>pulled up</u> all the <u>awful</u> flowers and <u>planted</u> <u>thistles</u> and <u>stinging</u> <u>nettles</u> and made it quite clear to the lawn that if it didn't stop growing, it was <u>con-crete</u> time. They buried their <u>various</u> <u>dead</u> and <u>semidead</u> friends and relations in the back-yard and trained the front gate to <u>keep out</u> <u>unwanted</u> visitors.

People usually cross the road rather than walk by the gate. The <u>mailman</u> has delivered letters with a long pair of barbecue tongs ever

12

since the day the mailbox ate his watch.

Underneath the house the Floods created a vast maze of cellars and tunnels that reach out in all directions for hundreds of yards. The lowest level is so deep underground you can feel the heat from the center of the earth and actually fry an egg on the floor.

And around the edge of the garden they

planted a tall, thick vicious hedge that keeps
out most prying eyes, though not all, as we
shall see later.

The Floods are a happy, loving family, and
they think their house is perfect. The problem
is everyone else.

Ordinary people don't like things to be different. Ordinary people want everyone to have
the same things they've got: the same car, the
same wide-screen television, the same barbecue,
and the same 2.4 children. Then they can go to
the supermarket and all feel the same, and all
talk about the TV show they watched last night
and where they're all going on their vacations.

In fact it's not quite that simple. Secretly most
people want to be exactly the same as everyone
else—only a bit better. They want their car to be
the one with the luxury bits and a bigger engine,

14

and they want their children to be better at school, and they want to have more money and a spa bath that all their neighbors haven't got.

So really, everyone is _jealous_ of everyone else.

Except the Floods.

They don't even have a car. If they want to go anywhere, either they travel by turbo-broomsticks that go so fast ordinary people can't see them,[4] or else they walk or take a taxi. Apart from Betty, they never go on the bus because people complain about the smell, which isn't so much bad as weird, like roses

---

[4] _You know how sometimes you think you see something out of the corner of your eye and when you turn around there's nothing there? Well, that's one of the Floods going by. Even if you had eyes in the back of your head and didn't blink, you still wouldn't be able to see them because they travel faster than the speed of light._

mixed with pepper and wet dog. And if they want a spa bath, they take off their clothes and stand in the backyard while their three black clouds rain on them. Not cold rain like what you and I would get, but warm rain that even has shampoo and conditioner in it.

So while everyone on the block thinks the Floods are strange, scary, and different and never invite them to their coffee mornings or Tupperware parties, the Floods are probably happier than all of them. Apart from the eldest son, Valla, they don't even go out to work, because they have everything they need without having to.

MONDAY MORNING, 5:30 A.M.

As the morning light peeped in through the bloodred curtains, the Floods' alarm snake bit Mordonna on the neck and woke her up. An alarm snake is like an alarm clock except it doesn't make any noise and it wakes you up by biting you on the neck. (That means it isn't actually like an alarm clock at all, except it does wake you up and it does alarm you.)

17

The big advantage of the alarm snake is that it wakes up only the person it bites, so someone else in the bed can stay fast asleep. If you are a normal human, it doesn't wake you up so much as kill you because it's very poisonous.

Nerlin was lying on his back with his mouth open, snoring like a hippopotamus that had just swallowed a rusty steam train. The alarm snake licked the sleep from Mordonna's eyes and slithered into the next room to wake Valla. Mordonna checked herself in the mirror to see if she was still as beautiful as she had been when she had gone to bed, and then she went downstairs to start the day.

"Come on, everyone," she shouted as she went downstairs. "Time to get up, time to get ready for school."

There were seven children and only one

bathroom, so there were the usual fights over who got in first, just like in normal houses. Everyone tried to get there before Merlinmary because it could take her up to an hour to do her hair, on account of the fact that it covers every square inch of her body. She even has hair on her eyeballs and tongue. While she is in the bathroom, though, she charges up all the electric razors and toothbrushes.

Breakfast in the Flood house is probably a bit different from your house. Vlad, the cat, hung around under the kitchen table, rubbing against someone's leg. No one ever discovered where the leg had come from or who it belonged to, but it was there every morning.

There was a lot more running around than in normal houses. Not because the children were out of control, but because their breakfasts kept trying to get away from them.

"Morbid, Silent, stop juggling your breakfast and just eat it," snapped Mordonna.

"Yeah, but look, Mom, we can make it stick to the ceiling," said Morbid. Silent simply nodded vigorously and grunted. He always thinks exactly the same as his twin and can't see the point in just repeating everything Morbid says.

"Anyone can make slugs stick to the ceiling, dear. Just eat them up while they're still nice and slimy."

Of course there was always at least one slug that slid out of the bread and vanished under the stove.

"Betty, stop teasing the sugar bats," said Mordonna. "Just put them in the warm milk and eat them up, or you'll have to go back to baby food."

The trouble was that Betty wasn't really old enough for sugar bats. She was only ten, and her hands were too small to hold the special spoon. So every time she scooped one up and held it to her mouth, it flew off and hid behind the fridge.

Vlad, the cat, added to the general chaos by leaping about on the kitchen counters, trying to catch the bats, as of course he never did.

After breakfast Vlad always felt depressed for an hour or so. He had no problem ripping little birds to bits, but he had never once caught a bat. No one thought to tell him that sugar bats have radar and could see him coming.

Winchflat and Merlinmary didn't do much better. Their rats' brains were so slippery they kept falling on the floor and slithering off to join the slugs under the stove.

"Oh, for goodness' sake, children, if you don't stop messing around, I'm just going to make you eat cornflakes," said Mordonna, tipping Satanella's morning entrails into her bowl by the back door. Satanella always had her meals right next to the cat flap so she could make a quick exit into the garden. Quite often she had to throw her food up and eat it again several times before she could finally manage to keep it down.

"Yeuuuwww, cornflakes," said Morbid.

"Gross," said Betty.

By the time each of the six youngest children had caught their breakfast and either eaten it or sucked its insides out, there was barely time to wipe the slime off their chins[5] before the wizard school bus materialized in one of the cellars.

"Come on, kids, hurry up. The bus will be here in a minute," Mordonna told them all. "Tangle your hair, and do make sure you've got dirt under every single one of your fingernails. I don't want the other parents thinking I don't bring you up properly."

---

[5] *And wring out the sponge into a bowl for the night eels' breakfast. (See the back of the book for information about the night eels and other Flood family pets.)*

"Mom, Satanella's eaten my homework," said Merlinmary.

"Well, she'll just have to bring it up again when you get to school," her mother replied. "And, Morbid, do remember to lock your schoolbag. I don't want your lunch crawling out and biting the bus driver again."

There are two reasons the bus appears in the cellar. First, that's where the bus stop is, and second, the bus that takes five of the children to school is not an ordinary bus, so if it did appear in the street outside the Floods' house, it would scare the living daylights out of the neighbors. The school is a special wizard and witch school, hidden away from the normal world in a secret valley right up in the mountains in darkest

Patagonia. To reach the school each day, Satanella, Merlinmary, Winchflat, and the twins have to cross several oceans, some of which can get very angry. They also travel over a desert or two, through fifty-foot _snowdrifts_, up a tall waterfall, and across a _bottomless_ lake. All of which, of course, an ordinary bus would find a bit difficult to do. In fact an ordinary bus wouldn't get more than twenty feet across the sea before _sinking_.

The wizard school bus, on the other hand, covers all these vast distances in nine minutes. To call the wizard bus a bus is stretching the _definition_ of the word "bus." The wizard bus is not so much a bus as it is a dragon with seats and a toilet.

♦ ♦ ♦

At last the house grew quiet again. Mordonna checked herself in the mirror. "Still staggeringly beautiful," she said, and sat down with a huge cup of strong coffee.

The remaining Flood child, Valla, finally came downstairs. He had the good sense to stay in bed cuddling his pet vampire bats, Nigel and Shirley, until the other kids were out of the house. Then he got up and spent a relaxed ten minutes in the bathroom, bleaching his face, before going downstairs for a quick cup of milkman's blood.[6] He then took the unknown leg from under the kitchen table

---

[6] *Valla believed that because milkmen always get up very early, if he drank some milkman's blood for breakfast, it would wake him up and get his day off to a bright start.*

and gave it to Nigel and
Shirley to <u>chew on</u> while he
was at work.

Valla was the manager of
the local blood bank. To him,
his job was like he died and
went to heaven. He loved his
work so much that he often
took it home with him. Both
his bedroom and his underground playroom were <u>littered</u>
<u>with</u> bags of blood, <u>labeled</u> and
<u>cataloged</u> like fine wines. His
favorite blood was the <u>rare</u>
type OOH+, which came
from only one person in the
whole world, a beautiful
Australian singer with a

very famous bottom. Valla had just one small bag of her blood, which he drank one drop at a time and only on very special occasions. To cover up the fact that he was taking more blood out of the blood bank than people were putting in, he replaced it with fake blood made out of tomato sauce, frog's spit, and a rare plant root from Tristan da Cunha. Most of the time this worked fine, and patients receiving Valla's fake blood hardly ever turned hyperactive or dropped dead.

MONDAY MORNING, 8:30 A.M.

Peace had descended briefly on the house. The alarm snake, having recovered from the headache it always got after biting Valla, slithered back into the parents' bedroom to wake up Nerlin, who had just come to the best bit of his dream.[7]

"Morning, handsome," said Mordonna as her husband stumbled into the kitchen. "How are we feeling today? Good night's sleep?"

"Mmm," Nerlin mumbled. "My mouth tastes like a very old washing machine full of dirty socks."

"That's nice, dear. Want some coffee?"

"In a minute. I'm still enjoying the socks."

"Good dreams?"

"Oh, yes," said Nerlin. "My favorite."

"Oh, the one with the, er . . . ?"

"Yes."

"And the big pink . . . ?"

---

[7] *Which my editor said I'm not allowed to tell you about. So I'm afraid you'll just have to make up Nerlin's dream yourself.*

"That's the one," said Nerlin. "I just love that dream, and you know, it never gets boring."

"Well, it wouldn't, would it?" Mordonna said. "Was I wearing the shiny thing?"

"Absolutely. Think I'd better have that coffee now."

The peace didn't last long. A few minutes later the thump, thump, thump of disco music mixed with shouting and swearing drifted over from the house next door. Then the neighbors' dog started barking, a big thundering bark that made the cups rattle.

You know how when everything seems perfect and you think life just couldn't get any better, something always spoils it? This was the something that did that to the Floods.

The neighbors from hell, the Dents.

"Mmm, not even nine o'clock. They're starting early today," said Mordonna, getting up from her chair.

"Yes," Nerlin agreed. "We'll have to do something about it. It's really getting on my nerves."

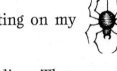

"No point in phoning the police. They never do anything."

"No, no, we'll sort it out ourselves."

"Well, I'm off to do the housework," said Mordonna, "see that the spiders are working properly."

"Yes, I'll take care of the mold and then the pets. I suppose it's pointless asking if the kids fed them?"

"As if."

With the Dents' noise echoing through the house, Mordonna went from room to room, checking for <u>cobwebs</u>. Where there weren't any, she left fresh spiders with detailed weaving patterns, and to encourage them, she put a few <u>juicy</u> bluebottles in with them.

Nerlin went down into the cellars to check the <u>damp</u> and spray the walls with a hose to make sure the mold stayed nice and healthy. Down on the third level he could still hear the Dents, a <u>muffled</u> <u>blur</u> of bangs and crashes. Then he fed the cellar pets: the night eels, the giant hipposlugs, and Doris, the three-hundred-and-fifty-year-old blind dodo. Of course, as in most families, the pets belonged to the children, who always forgot to look after them, so their parents had to. Cleaning out the litter <u>tray</u> of a three-hundred-and-fifty-year-old blind dodo was not a job for the <u>faint-hearted</u> or anyone with a good sense of smell.

By the time Nerlin staggered outside and tipped the contents over the veggie garden he felt pretty faint and had to sit on Mordonna's mother's grave and breathe deeply for a few minutes.[8]

"Morning, Mother-in-law. How are the maggots wriggling?" he asked, and the mound of earth beneath him shivered in reply as Queen Scratchrot twitched her bones.

"Oh, well. I'd better get on with things," said Nerlin.

After the cobwebs Mordonna went back through every room, checking that the dust was properly organized: not too thick on the tabletops and nicely gathered into hairy piles

---

[8] *It has to be said, though, that where Nerlin emptied Doris's litter tray, the lettuce grew two feet tall.*

in the corners. By the time she did that the kitchen frogs had clambered over the dirty dishes and licked them clean, the crusty toad had nibbled all the hard burned bits off the pans, and the cutlery snake had slithered his tongue between every prong of every fork. All Mordonna had to do was put everything back in the cupboards.

The noise from next door always faded a bit after lunch. That was when Mr. Dent, after a hard morning of shouting and swearing and a thick, greasy lunch, fell asleep and Mrs. Dent settled down to watch a reality show full of people that made even her look good.

Nerlin and Mordonna took advantage of the temporary peace by having an afternoon nap, doing a bit of gardening, and trimming Grandma's toenails where they grew out of

35

her grave by the clothesline. Then it was teatime, followed by another short snooze before the kids came home from school.

If it hadn't been for the wretched Dents next door, life would have been perfect.

When the Floods moved into number 13 Acacia Avenue, there had been two nice old couples in the houses on either side. Life had been peaceful. Their neighbors had brought them cake, and in return the Floods had given them crispy fried cockroaches. One of the advantages of having old people for neighbors is that they often can't see very well, so when the Flood children gave them bowls of crispy fried cockroaches, which are delicious, by the way, they thought they were bits of crispy bacon.

The disadvantage of having old people for neighbors is that they die a lot. Even when Winchflat, who was the scientific brains of the Flood family, had used his Massive-Electric-Shock-Dead-Person-iReviver[9] on the old couple at number 11, they only came back to life for a few weeks.

That was when the Dents moved in and shattered the calm of the whole street.

They were the neighbors from hell. Not real hell, where some of the Floods' best friends lived, but hell on earth, which isn't actually a real place, more a state of mind. If you think

---

[9] *See the back of the book for instructions on how to build your own.*

of the most horrible person you've ever met or seen on TV, the Dents were much worse than that.

The Dents fought each other and swore a lot in very loud voices. They filled their front yard with rusty old cars and broken machines and their backyard with thousands of empty bottles and other garbage, which often ended up in the Floods' garden. In one of the old cars out front, they kept a ferocious dog called Rambo that tried to bite everyone.

All their clothes were made of shiny nylon, and Mr. Dent had a terrible mustache and a big gold chain. Mrs. Dent thought she still had the same legs she'd had at seventeen and liked to wear her skirts as short as she'd done then. This scared a lot of people, especially small children, who would take one look at her knobbly knees approaching them at eye level and burst into tears.

Mr. Dent's job was making sure he never had a job, which there wasn't much chance of anyway. When he was eighteen, he had been sent to work cleaning out the pipes at the sewerage works, but he was fired after two days because the pipes were more disgusting after he'd been inside them than they had been before. That had taken a lot of sneaky skill on his part, but to make extra sure he was never given a job again, he slipped in the sludge and hurt his back just enough to be paid a large amount of money to keep him from taking the company to court for damages. Once word spread about this, no one would ever give him a job again.

While it appeared that Mr. Dent was a lazy bum who spent all day sleeping and drinking, he did in fact have a secret hobby that took up a lot of his time. It wasn't the sort of hobby you joined a club to do or one that involved any real skill or talent.

Mr. Dent stole cars.

Or to be precise, Mr. Dent stole bits of cars. When he was younger, he had stolen whole cars, but now he just took parts of cars. There was no logic to it. He didn't take them to sell to anyone else or use on his own car. Nor did he take the same parts all the time. One week he would collect left-hand mirrors. The next week he would take the knobs off gearshifts or the pieces of pipe that connected the

41

windshield washer bottles to the nozzles. It was simply that he was too lazy to take the whole car anymore.

On his last birthday Mr. Dent had gotten an old Sherman tank. It sat in his front yard on top of three old cars, a small oak tree, and a large part of Mr. Dent's empty beer bottle collection. As far as the Floods were concerned, this was good news and bad news. The bad news was that it was louder than all of Mr. Dent's old cars and motorbikes added together. It had wrecked the pavement when it had arrived, and when he had nothing else to do (which was most of the time), Mr. Dent used to get inside the tank and start the engine. There was always the risk that he might drive it over his neighbors' houses, so to be on the safe side, Mordonna put a spell on the tank that made all the metal tracks rust together so it could never be moved again.

"Why didn't you just break the engine, so we don't have to listen to it anymore?" asked Nerlin.

"I thought about it," said Mordonna, "but I reckoned that if the engine stopped working, he might get something even bigger and noisier."

The good news was that when the tank's engine was running, the Floods could no longer hear most of the other noises the Dents were making. Mrs. Dent of course was loud enough to be heard over anything.

As the months passed, Mr. Dent screwed, welded, and glued all the things he had stolen from the town's cars onto his tank until it looked like something out of the Museum of Modern Art. Several pretentious people actually tried to buy the tank, one offering more than one hundred thousand dollars, but Mr. Dent thought they were government spies from the unemployment agency trying to trick him, and he sent them packing.

Mrs. Dent also had an activity she referred to as her little hobby. She took her son, Dickie, down to the corner store and slapped him around the head. While he was screaming as loudly as he could, Mrs. Dent used the distraction to nip behind the counter and steal cigarettes.

"Couldn't you just pretend to slap me, Mom?" Dickie asked.

"No, of course not. You wouldn't make a loud enough noise," said his mom. "Besides, a good slap never hurt anyone."

"It hurts *me*," said Dickie.

"Well, I'm sure you deserve it. My mom used to hit me, and it never did me any harm."

This was not true. The harm bit, that is, not the hitting bit. That was true. Mrs. Dent's mom had hit her so often that it had turned her from a really horrible little girl who pulled the wings off ladybugs into a really, really horrible big girl who pulled the wings off seagulls.

If Mrs. Dent had not been hit as a child, she could well have ended up a much nicer person who would have bought cigarettes on the cheap instead of stealing them.[10]

Mrs. Dent's main job was avoiding Mr. Dent and anything that kept her away from the TV.

They had two vile children: Tracylene, who had way too many boyfriends, way too much eyeliner, and way too few brain cells, and Dickie, who was ten but should never have been allowed to become one, never mind two, three, four, etc. Dickie's hobby was breaking into other people's houses, peeing on their furniture, and putting Barbie dolls in their microwaves.

---

[10] *Which just goes to prove you should never hit children or adults or goldfish or anything alive, not even geography teachers.*

If crime were in the *Guinness World Records*, Dickie Dent would have had an entry as the youngest person ever to have been given community service. He was actually below the minimum legal age for such punishment by several years and was given it only because there was no other option. Normally a child as disruptive as Dickie from such a dysfunctional family is taken into foster care, but after several failed attempts at this—he had tried to eat his last caretaker—there was no one who was prepared to take him on, so he was left with his parents. The authorities were left with few choices: send him to the zoo or to jail or make him do community service. The last time he was hauled into court, he had tried to microwave a Barbie doll while it was still being firmly held on to by a small girl—he had come up before one of those judges who liked to give people a second chance after they had been given a fifteenth chance and still blown it, so instead of sending the evil Dickie to the zoo where he belonged, she had given him community service.[11]

Dickie was in the same class as Betty Flood, and when he wasn't stealing other kids' lunch money, he used to sit behind her and pull her hair and call her names.

Betty was the only Flood child who didn't go to the wizard school. To try to make her less wizardy, Mordonna sent Betty to the nor-

---

[11] *A shortsighted judge, thinking Dickie was a very small adult and not a small boy, had actually sent him to a grown-ups' jail when he was eight years old. Until the mistake was discovered, it had been the happiest week of Dickie's life, and he had learned lots of new and exciting things, like forgery and safecracking.*

mal school a few streets away. Betty would have preferred to go to the same school as her brothers and sisters. Normal people, if you could call Dickie Dent and other kids in her class normal, were so dull. None of them could see in the dark or even make a pencil move without using their hands.

When she started school, Betty had decided that no matter how many lessons her parents made her take, she would stay different. Not

that she had any choice in the matter. Boring facts went in her left ear and rushed out of the right one as quickly as they could. Betty couldn't even learn her nine times table. This was not because she was dumb but because Betty knew that these things weren't important.

"You're a witch," Dickie hissed at Betty when the teacher wasn't looking.

"Don't think that saying nice things is going to make me like you," said Betty, and she made a huge pimple swell up on his forehead.

"Teacher, teacher," Dickie cried, "she's given me a pimple."

"Dickie Dent, don't be absurd," said the teacher. "People can't give you pimples."

Betty would probably have stood out less if she had eaten ordinary school lunches instead of pickled lizards and toads' knees. She did try eating the school meat pies and turkey twizzlers once, but they only made her ill.

"You're weird," said Bridie McTort, the school bully, but Betty thought that was a compliment.

"Why's that?" asked Betty, looking all innocent.

"Eating lizards and frogs, that's gross, that is," she said.

"See your burger?"

"Yeah?"

"This is what it's made of," said Betty, and a huge smelly pile of gross animal bits appeared on the table.

Bridie felt that retching thing in her throat where you try really hard not to throw up but know that nothing will stop it, and she did, all over the floor.

For good measure, Betty gave her big uncomfortable pimples on her bottom, so no matter how she sat down, it hurt.

"See?" Betty said. "All that dreadful food gives you pimples too."

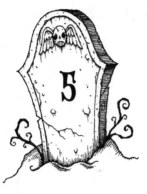

Lots of people hate their jobs. It's a part of their lives that is necessary to make money to buy food and houses and clothes. While they're at work, they dream of the time when they won't be at work, when they'll be with their loved ones, having a life. They dream of their hobbies, which are often like work, except people enjoy them.

Some lucky people actually enjoy their jobs,

or to put it another way, some people actually love what they do all day. Mrs. Dent loved being <u>hypnotized</u> by TV. She had a TV at the foot of the bed that she turned on as soon as she woke up. She had a waterproof TV in the shower and a tiny TV to look at as she went downstairs. Mr.

Dent loved what he did all day, which was nothing plus eating plus drinking plus sleeping.

As for the Floods, they would have been happy all of the time if it hadn't been for the Dents.

Like most families, the Floods had hobbies that they loved. Under their house in the vast network of cellars, each Flood had a few rooms of their own where they could play or experiment to their heart's content. When the Floods were doing their favorite things, and even on the rare occasions when there was not much noise coming from the Dents' house, the Dents were still there, niggling away at the back of everyone's mind. Even when the family was down in the deepest cellars, seven floors below the house, the Dents managed to spoil things.

Winchflat, the family genius, had a whole

55

floor of cellars jam-packed with incredible equipment, where he invented things that normal people would have shouted about and got very rich as a result of. Winchflat made a tiny pill that you put into water that would make a car go. He hadn't bothered to tell anyone about it because he always knew he could invent something better—like the car he was working on that could hover just above the ground, read your mind, and take you to wherever you wanted to go and not actually need the water with the pill in it to make it work because it all was powered by one single bumblebee and a dandelion. If it hadn't been for the endless drone of Mrs. Dent's TV in the background, he would have had the whole thing finished. But that noise took the edge off his concentration.

In another cellar Merlinmary was charging

the batteries. Her hair was so full of electricity that at night she slept in a lead-lined room with her fingers pushed into a special socket that charged up a huge bank of batteries, enough to run the whole house. She was born with this talent because the night Nerlin made her in the laboratory down in his cellar, using a recipe he hadn't tried before, there was a terrible storm like those you get in Frankenstein movies. The difference was that Nerlin did not need a bolt of lightning to bring Merlinmary to life; he needed only a teaspoon of peanut butter. So when the lightning hit the house that night fifteen years before, racing down into the cellars and up the legs of the laboratory bench[12] at the very moment Nerlin

---

[12] *The lightning also ran up Nerlin's legs, but he quite liked that.*

was bringing Merlinmary to life, it had filled the child with enough electricity to run the whole of America for seventy-five years.[13]

In fact Merlinmary had so much electricity inside her that she made the meter run backward, meaning that every time the Floods got a power bill, the electricity company had to give them money.

Because of the distraction of Mr. Dent's revving up his clapped-out motorbikes, Merlinmary sometimes lost concentration and put her fingers in the socket backward. This used to make her hair all frizzy and sometimes give half the town a blackout. With the Dents getting louder and louder because of the

---

[13] *This calculation is based on only 36.72 percent of the population using electric toothbrushes, so it could be a few years more or less.*

Sherman tank, this was happening more and
more.

Morbid and Silent bred beautiful moths in
one of their rooms. They fed the baby cater-
pillars on the finest orchid petals and tucked
their chrysalises up in tiny beds of cotton. The
twins helped the baby moths emerge safely
into the world and then pulled their wings off
and ate them. (The wings, that is, not the
moths—that would be disgusting.) Sometimes
the Dents would start a shouting match, and
the twins would throw away the wings and
eat the moths, making them very sick.

Betty spent many happy hours making false
wings for all the damaged moths that kept
crawling under her door. She made them by
boiling up cockroaches, spreading the sticky
liquid out on a sheet of glass, and cutting it

59

into little wings. When Mrs. Dent threw saucepans around, Betty lost her place and forgot how many times she had wound up the rubber band to make the wings work, and the moths would snap in half.

Valla, even though he was obsessed with blood—so much that he often took his own blood out to look at it under a microscope—had a soft spot for cockroaches and had a cellar with a tiny orphanage for all the baby cockroaches that had lost their parents in Betty's saucepan. His favorite bit was trying to give the cockroaches blood transfusions, which required complete silence and very great concentration. Once again the noise from the Dents' house distracted him, and a lot of cockroaches exploded.

Winchflat loved the stars and

60

planets and spent hours looking at them, very difficult from a cellar seven floors below-ground. Instead of doing the obvious thing as you or I would—which is to go outside or up on the roof—Winchflat got around the problem by actually bringing the stars down to him. He invented a fantastically powerful space vacuum cleaner that could suck whole galaxies out of the sky and into a bottle on his bench. He was a well-brought-up, tidy child, so naturally, when he finished looking at the galaxies, he always put them back. Always, that is, except when a sudden explosion from the Dents' backyard—Dickie playing with matches in the shed after eating three cans of baked beans—made Winchflat press button B *before* button A. The result was that a galaxy that should have been in the Milky Way was now on the opposite

side of space, and it was upside down too.

Even Satanella had a cellar. In the middle of
the floor there was a tree. First she would go
sniff it; then she would chase a cat up it. This
was not Vlad, of course, but a special cat from
Rent-a-Scaredy-Cat. Satanella then sat by the
door, waiting for the cat to try to escape, as it
always did when Satanella got distracted by a
sudden noise, such as Dickie's exploding again.

Mordonna kept offering to turn Satanella
back into a little girl, but Satanella always
refused, saying, "Life is so simple when you're
a dog. Eat, sleep, chase cats. That's it. Oh, and
a bit of a tickle behind the ear, and of course
stick and ball chasing. It doesn't get any better
than that." Still, there were times she wished
she were a girl again, so that she could go and
thump Dickie.

Winchflat had made Satanella a Stick-and-Red-Rubber-Ball-Throwing Machine, which she kept in a very long, narrow dungeon. No one else would admit it, but every single one of her brothers and sisters and her parents played with the machine when they thought no one else was looking.[14] It was one of those family secrets that everyone else knew about but they all pretended they didn't. I suppose it proves that it's true when people say, "There is a bit of dog in all of us."[15]

Nerlin and Mordonna shared a cellar, but you're not old enough to know what it's for. Orange jelly, chains, socks, mugs of hot choco-

---

[14] *Winchflat made himself a Beep-Loudly-When-Anyone-Else-Is-Coming Machine so he would NEVER get caught chasing red rubber balls.*

[15] *Editor: No one says that.*

late, and a big armchair were involved (though not necessarily in that order), but even their hobby was spoiled by the Dents' noise.

SUNDAY AFTERNOON, 3:42 P.M.—

FAMILY MEETING

"Something has to be done," said Nerlin.

"You can see why their name is Dent," said Valla. "They are a <u>dent</u> on the face of humanity."

"Yeah," everyone agreed.

"And what do you do to dents?" Betty asked.

"You fill them in," said Winchflat.

"But not before you've bashed them as flat as you can first," said Morbid. Silent nodded.

"Grr," said Satanella, thinking how nice it would be to chew on a Dent leg bone.

"Couldn't we just put a 'be nice' spell on

them?" asked Betty.

"Well, darling, I don't think there's one powerful enough to fix all their horrendous problems," said Mordonna. "I remember when I was young, my mother tried one on some terrible people who were eating her best friend's children, and it ended really badly."

"What happened?"

"They all turned into history teachers," said Mordonna. "No, it's way too risky."

"We want them out of our town," said Winchflat.

"Galaxy," said Valla.

"I think you should go talk to them before we do anything," said Mordonna.

"Okay, my dear, but it won't do any good," said Nerlin. "You can't reason with people like that."

"I'll come with you, Dad," said Merlinmary. "If there's any trouble, I can give them an electric shock."

The Dents had turned their front yard into a pigsty, except no decent pig would ever have wanted to live there. There were three rusty old cars, now half buried beneath the Sherman tank—one where Rambo, the dog, lived, another where Tracylene locked up her boyfriends to keep them from running away, and another where Mr. Dent fell asleep when he couldn't find his own front door. In between the cars the grass grew a foot high, burying all the trash that never quite made it to the garbage cans.

As Nerlin and Merlinmary walked through the hole in the wall that had once been a gate,

Rambo lifted his head and growled. He had a thick spiked collar around his neck and a heavy chain padlocked to the steering wheel. His eyes flashed like burning coals, but it was hard to be sure he was looking at you because he was seriously cross-eyed. His sight was so wonky that he'd bitten his own leg quite a few times when he thought he was attacking the postman.

"What do you want?" said Mr. Dent as Nerlin and Merlinmary stood on his front step. "Nark off, freaks."

"There's no need to be like that," said Nerlin. "We'd just like to have a talk."

"I said nark off, you weirdos, or I'll sic Rambo on you."

"I wouldn't do that if I were

you," Nerlin told him.

"Oh, yeah?" said Mr. Dent. "Why not?"

"I just wouldn't," said Nerlin.

Mr. Dent unclipped Rambo's chain. The crazy dog was so desperate to get at Nerlin that he knocked Mr. Dent flying, covering him in drool and dog breath, but before he could reach Nerlin, Merlinmary snapped her fingers, and the giant rottweiler turned into a tiny poodle. As Mr. Dent struggled to get up, Rambo, the poodle, shot up the inside of his trouser leg and bit him.

"You narkin' . . ." Mr. Dent began, but he couldn't finish his sentence as Rambo bit him again, shot down his other trouser leg, and raced inside the house. Mr. Dent staggered to his feet and walked straight into the back bumper of Rambo's car.

"You, you, you," he spluttered, and crawled indoors, where Rambo was waiting to pay him back some more for all the kicks and swearing Mr. Dent had given him over the years. As Rambo raced through every room in the Dents' house, getting his revenge, it became clear why the first half of the word "poodle" is "poo."

Small dogs can run a lot faster than big, clumsy dogs or people. So the big, clumsy Dents had no chance of catching Rambo, no matter how hard they tried, especially as Rambo was about three times more intelligent than they were.

"Nice one, <u>sweetheart</u>," Nerlin said to his daughter as they left. "First round to us, I think."

The next day, when the Dent children were at school and Mrs. Dent was in her usual place in front of the TV, watching *Dr. Clint's Trailer Trash Special*, and Mr. Dent was still asleep in bed, Rambo, the poodle, lay in Dickie's bed. Rambo fell asleep and dreamed of the days when he'd been a puppy with all his brothers and sisters. Life had been good then, those first three months. Then he had gone to live with the Dents, and it had all been downhill after that. After all those years of being chained up in a wrecked car, it was warm and cozy in Dickie's bed.

Dickie had always been scared out of his wits by Rambo when the dog was a rottweiler. When Dickie was a baby, his dad's idea of a good laugh had been to hold him inches away from the ferocious dog's drooling fangs. Dickie hated Rambo, and Rambo hated Dickie. The boy was the worst one in the family. The others just ignored him, but Dickie teased him. It was his job to feed Rambo, and quite often he would deliberately put the food

73

bowl down a bit farther than the dog's chain would let him reach. Sometimes he would spit on the food, or soak Rambo with the garden hose or throw sticks at him. Rambo hated Dickie so much he had actually pulled the car he was chained to halfway across the garden and made a groove in the back of his neck that gave him headaches.

Dickie, of course being a total coward, always made sure he kept out of Rambo's reach.

Now Rambo was free, and he wanted revenge. He shook himself awake and went outside, where he dug under his car and hauled out his favorite bone, not the really old one that was almost a fossil, but the one that still had some blood on it and a large family of maggots living a happy and meaningful life in the marrow. Now that he was a small poodle, the bone looked enormous, and it took Rambo most of the morning to drag it upstairs and bury it again in Dickie's bed.

That night, as Dickie began to fall asleep, the maggots crawled out of the bone and between Dickie's toes. Because the words "Dickie" and "bath" were not used in the same sentence more than once a month, Dickie was used to itching and scratching. What he wasn't used to was the itchy bits moving about.

He threw back the sheets and screamed, "Mommmm!"

Mrs. Dent, as usual, was tuned out of the real world. She had just switched channels to watch the *Big Brother Special Shock Edition*, where some brain cells had been discovered in one of the <u>contestants</u>, and the <u>viewers</u> had to guess who they belonged to.

"It's them Floods' fault," Dickie cried. "If they hadn't done that to Rambo, he'd still be chained up outside."

As he stood crying in the shower, he decided he would wait until the Floods went out and then break into their house and get his revenge. With a towel tied around his face to keep out the smell, he rolled Rambo's bone into a plastic bag.

As well as being a mean and <u>nasty</u> little boy, Dickie Dent was very, very stupid. He was too stupid to <u>realize</u> that the last place on earth you should break into was a house that belonged to a family of witches and wizards. He waited until he saw the family leave the house for their evening walk in the local graveyard; then he kicked a hole in the fence and crawled through it and squeezed under the hedge into the Floods' backyard. The back door was unlocked, so he slipped inside.

Part of Dickie's being very, very stupid was the fact that he couldn't count. When he saw the Floods go out, he hadn't made sure all nine of them were there. What made him very, very, *very* stupid was that the Flood who hadn't gone out was the one he actually went to school with.

The house felt creepy. The air was cold and damp, even though outside, it was a warm day. There weren't any empty french fry containers or half-eaten burgers with mold on them like in his own kitchen. The whole place smelled horrible.

It smelled really, really old with a hint of

dog bone that made Dickie feel ill.

Right, Dickie thought, *time for revenge.*

He walked over to the oven and put Rambo's bone on the top rack.

But he was not alone. As he knelt on the floor and reached into the oven to light the gas, Betty, who had heard Dickie kicking in the fence, tiptoed into the kitchen. Just as he was about to strike the match, Betty said, "Hello, Dickie. Have you come to cook our dinner for us?"

The lid flew off a jar of pickled frogs' eyes in fish oil on the counter, and it tipped itself over Dickie's head. The breakfast creatures that had been hiding under the stove slithered forward.

"I'm—I'm—I'm not scared of you," he cried.

"Well, you should be."

"You're just a dumb witch," Dickie sniveled.

"Witch, yes," said Betty. "Dumb, no."

Betty snapped her fingers, and the pickled frogs' eyes slithered down Dickie's face onto his T-shirt. Dickie tried to get up, but the floor was wet with fish oil, and he kept slipping.

"You wait till I tell my dad," he cried.

"What?" said Betty. "Tell him some pickled fish eyes stared at you?"

Betty, who was really a very kind, sweet girl who helped old spiders across the road even if she did eat them when they got to the other side, thought she should feel a bit sorry for Dickie. But he was so horrible to her and to all the other kids at school who were smaller than he was that she didn't.

"Are you scared?" she asked.

"N-n-n-n-no," Dickie lied, trying to get to the door. Betty snapped her fingers again, and the slimy stuff Dickie was lying in began to get hot. He couldn't pretend any longer. He was terrified.

"You can say sorry now," said Betty.

"I'm sorry," Dickie cried out.

"You are a nasty, evil little boy, aren't you?"

said Betty. "Breaking into people's houses and doing nasty things and being vile to everyone."

"Yes. I'm sorry," Dickie whimpered.

"And you're a liar too, aren't you?"

"Yes . . . sorry," cried Dickie.

"And that's the main problem, really," said Betty. "You keep saying sorry, but you're probably lying."

"No, I'm not, really," said Dickie.

"Really?"

"Really."

The fish oil stopped getting hot, and Dickie grabbed hold of a chair and pulled himself up.

"Can I go now?" he said.

"Promise you won't be evil anymore?" said Betty.

"Yes," said Dickie with his fingers crossed

behind his back. But he was still just as stupid as before, and when he turned toward the door, he still had them crossed, and Betty saw them.

"Stop," she snapped, and Dickie's feet stuck to the floor.

"What?"

"Be afridge," said Betty. "Be very afridge."

Dickie laughed that nasty little snigger that mean little boys all over the world do so well. "Don't you mean 'be *afraid*'?" He sneered.

"I know what I mean," said Betty. She *had* actually meant to say, "Be afraid," but as often happens when people get excited, she had got her words a bit muddled up, though there was no way she was going to let Dickie know *that*.

Very slowly Dickie felt himself getting squarer. It didn't hurt at all. Betty was a witch, but she could be quite kind and gentle. It was something she hoped to grow out of as she got older.

Dickie stood up, but he couldn't run away because his legs had sort of vanished. He still had feet; in fact he now had four of them, and they were self-leveling hydraulic feet. As he looked down for what would be the last time, he thought that he actually looked nicer made of stainless steel than he had made of skin and fat. He had a gorgeous ice cube maker in his left-hand door and a screen in the right that told you exactly what food you had inside, when you had bought it, and how much longer you would have to wait until it was nicely past its sell by date.

Dickie's last thought was: *Wow, I am, like, the handsomest, most expensive fridge in the shop. If only Mom could see me now.*

The last thing he said was: "Mmmmm-mmmmmmmmmmmmmmmmmmmmmmmmm-mmmmmmmmmmm," which he hummed in a very soft, expensive sort of way several times a day.

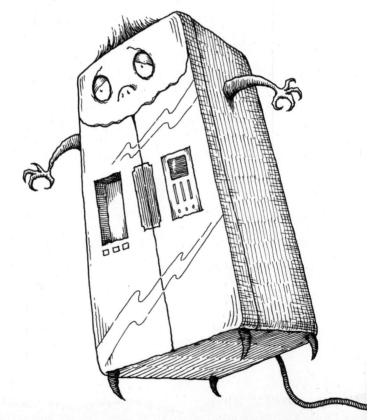

Betty decided that Dickie would probably be empty and have to charge up overnight to get cold, until she remembered that Dickie was a magic fridge. And when she peered inside, he was lovely and cold and full of her favorite food. In the freezer there were seventeen kinds of ice cream. In the fridge there was a huge plate of cold roast lamb with a two-liter jug of mint sauce. There were barbecued chicken wings, a sticky date pudding, and a very large box of chocolates with no hard toffees at all.

Betty took out a tub of delicious strawberry ice cream.

"Excellent," she said, as Vlad licked the last of the fish oil off the floor.

No one in Dickie's family noticed he was missing at first. Mr. and Mrs. Dent didn't like their children very much, and the less they saw of them, the more they liked it. Once, Tracylene had been in prison for a month for shoplifting, and her parents hadn't even noticed she'd been gone.

When Mrs. Dent stuck Dickie's burger, fries, and beans down on the table for dinner and realized she'd just put it on top of another plate of burger, fries, and beans, she wondered why her son hadn't eaten the night before. She shouted upstairs for him, but by the time she realized he hadn't answered, her favorite program was on TV, so she didn't bother.[16] The opening music was playing, and it drew her like a magnet toward the screen.

There were five plates of burger, fries, and beans piled on top of one another before she thought that maybe Dickie was not at home.

---

16 *Mrs. Dent's favorite TV program was* Mega-Extreme Celebrity Really Dumb Fat Ugly Idiot Loser Makeover, *where people who were dumber, fatter, and even more useless than Mrs. Dent were chopped up by very, very rich doctors and turned into really thin and not quite as ugly as before stupid idiots who couldn't believe they were still losers. It made Mrs. Dent feel a lot better about herself.*

"I wonder where he's gone to," she said as she sat down to watch TV again.

"Who?" said Mr. Dent. "Tracylene, get me something to drink." The fridge was in the hall, to be nearer to Mr. Dent's TV chair, but even then, it was too much of an effort for him to fetch his own drinks.

"Get it yourself," Tracylene shouted from her bedroom. "I'm going out, Mom."

"Don't do anything I wouldn't do," Mrs. Dent told her.

"You wish."

Tracylene was wearing her favorite outfit, although the endless diet of burgers, fries, and beans made it harder to fit into than she remembered.

"Must have shrunk in the wash," she said to herself as she checked her reflection in the mirror. "Still looking good, though."

This was a strange definition of "looking good." Large amounts of Tracylene bulged out above and below her bright pink miniskirt, and a large amount of her chest simply refused to stay where it was meant to. The fact that her spindly high-heeled shoes didn't collapse under her weight was proof that Chinese engineers are very clever people.

"Cheap underwear," she muttered, topping up her layers of eye shadow and lipstick.

"Cheap undies, cheap undies," squawked Adolf, the parakeet, the Dents' other pet. Adolf lived in Tracylene's bedroom, and she had taught him to talk.

Whenever Tracylene posed in front of her mirror, as she did dozens of times a day, Adolf would whistle at her and say, "More lipstick, baby!" and "Nice legs!" When he was alone, though, Adolf used to look in his mirror and say to his reflection, "It's a rotten job, but someone's got to do it." After all Tracylene was the only friend he had in the world apart from Adolf-in-the-mirror, who never had anything of his own to say.

Tracylene tottered out of the front door and went off

to meet her friends Shareelene and Torylene and a group of pimply boys who worshipped them.

After a few more days had gone by and the pile of cold burger, fries, and beans had grown to eight plates high, Mrs. Dent had an idea. Tomorrow she would put the ninth plate next to the old pile instead of on top of it, just in case the pile fell over. It was the most complicated thought she had that month.

"He hasn't been at school all week," she said the next night. "Do you think we should call the police?"

"Who? Why?" asked Mr. Dent. "Tracylene, get me something to drink."

"Get it yourself," said Tracylene. "I'm going out, Mom."

"Don't do anything I wouldn't do," said Mrs. Dent.

"You wish."

Tracylene had tried to imagine something her mother wouldn't do, but she couldn't.

Mrs. Dent called the police.

At first the police didn't want to go to the Dents' house.

"That family's been nothing but trouble since they moved here," Sergeant DaVinci said after he'd gotten off the phone. "The mother's been arrested for dangerous driving. The dad's been arrested for drunk and disorderly conduct. The daughter's been arrested for shoplifting, and the boy's always in trouble. They're bad news."

"Maybe if we keep quiet," his assistant said,

"they'll all vanish one by one."

"We can only hope so," said the sergeant.

But Mrs. Dent kept phoning every few days for the next month until the police could ignore her no longer. By the time they went around to number 11 Acacia Avenue, the kitchen table had forty-three plates of cold burger, fries, and beans piled up on it. Mrs. Dent had gotten it into her head that if she stopped putting Dickie's dinner out every day, she might never see him again.

"Okay, Mrs. Dent, when

did your little boy disappear?" DaVinci asked her.

"Um, one, two, three, four . . ."

Mrs. Dent tried to count the plates of cold food but got stuck when she reached seven. The sergeant could count to fifteen, which he did three times and then subtracted two.

"I haven't put today's dinner out yet," said Mrs. Dent, "so that's another day."

"Reumm, yurghhmm oh," said the sergeant with a mouthful of cold burger.

They took away the cold dinners for forensic examination, as well as the soda they found in the fridge—just in case there were finger-prints on the bottles.

"Don't you want to see Dickie's room?" said Mrs. Dent.

"Disgusting, untidy, smelly, red sports car

posters, dirty clothes, wet towels, unmade bed, broken toys, is it?" said DaVinci.

"Yes, don't you want to check it for DNA?"

"Mrs. Dent, we don't really do that. You've been watching too much TV."

"Don't be ridiculous," said Mrs. Dent. "How can anyone watch *too* much TV?"

"Whatever," said the sergeant, and left.

He thought about getting a missing persons poster made for Dickie, but he decided not to because it would frighten people.

8

In the meantime the Floods were enjoying their new fridge.

"It's much better than our old fridge," said Nerlin. "Top of the range, excellent."

"Nice one, little sister," said Valla. "High five."

"No, no, Valla. Remember what happened last time?" Mordonna asked him.

"What?" said Valla.

"Your hand fell off, and it took me ages to sew it back on again."

"Isn't that supposed to happen when you do a high five?" Valla asked.

"No, not usually."

Even Vlad, the cat, loved the new fridge. As he walked past it, he could see his reflection in the doors and pretend it was another cat stalking him. Also, inside, there was a special chilled fish tank full of Siamese fighting fish, his favorite meal.

It really was a magic fridge, with something just right for every single one of the Floods.

"Well done, sweetheart," Nerlin said to Betty. "We're all very proud of you."

"It's the best sort of recycling," said Winchflat. "Take something broken and useless, and turn it into something really useful. And I'm so glad you gave him that special finish so we never have to polish him. Stainless steel can be really hard to keep looking nice."

Dickie said nothing. He was a fridge, and fridges—even the most advanced ones—don't speak.[17] He just hummed softly in his expensive I'm-so-happy sort of way.

---

17 *Although I believe you'll soon be able to buy one that tells you when you need more milk or to throw out that piece of chicken that's past its sell by date and complains when you put inside it things it doesn't like, like dead dogs and parsnips.*

And because Dickie was a magic fridge, no matter how much of the wonderful food everyone ate, there was always more, though of course Mordonna still went shopping to buy ordinary things like milk and butter that Dickie the fridge thought he was too important to keep producing.

If you have ever been to a twenty-four-hour supermarket at two A.M, you know that a lot of the people you see there at that time of night probably live under stones and avoid daylight. If you go there on a Friday night, as well as these strange creatures, for whom shoes are something they've heard about but don't really believe in, you might see families of witches or wizards doing their shopping.

They always go on Friday nights because

Friday is the evil day of the week,[18] and it's the day when all the food near its sell by date is sold off cheap. When the Floods first moved to Acacia Avenue, Mordonna searched the town for the supermarket with the most stuff that was past its sell by date. This wasn't so she could save money, but as she said, "It isn't just wine and wizards that improve with age;

---

18 *It's actually Saturday morning.*

bacon gets better too."

Usually it was Mordonna and Betty who did the shopping. Most children are fast asleep at this time of night, but witches don't need the same rest each day that ordinary people do. Because witches and wizards often have really scary dreams, it's actually more relaxing for them to stay awake. So the night manager of the 9/13 supermarket was used to seeing

Betty there and never complained about her being up so late.

There was only one checkout line open and no one stocking the shelves on Friday nights because they all were too scared to do it when the witches were shopping. What they didn't realize was that witches and wizards are actually a lot nicer than many normal people because they don't have to prove they have the power by getting angry or self-important, but as always happens, people are judged by their clothes and faces, and witches do look scary.

The supermarket was where Mordonna first met the two other witches who lived in the town. There was the Drain family, who were nice and had a lot in common with the Floods. The other wizard family was the

Nauseous-Fletchers, who had very little in common with anyone because they were terrible snobs and would never have used the word "common" in any sentence at all.

"Excuse me," said Mordonna to the night manager, "can you tell me where the black-hearted beans are, please?"

The night manager, like most men, was enchanted with Mordonna's beauty and liked to move the things she bought every week so she would have to ask him where they were. Mordonna knew he was doing it but went along with it, because all she had to do was flutter her eyelids at him to get a 10 percent discount.

"F-f-f-f-fourth aisle, f-f-f-f-far end on the le-le-le-le-left," he stammered.

He had printed out a photo of Mordonna

from the store's security camera and spent hours at home trying to talk to it without stuttering, which he didn't do normally.

As Mordonna and Betty reached the back of the store, they saw a girl in a uniform pushing a cart around, stocking up the shelves.

"Mom," said Betty, "isn't that the girl from next door?"

"So it is," said Mordonna. "Who'd have guessed she'd actually have a job. Maybe she's not as bad as we thought."

Tracylene Dent pushed the cart through the door into the storeroom and a few minutes later came back with it empty. She went to the baked beans shelves and began putting cans *into* the cart.

"She's not filling up the shelves," Betty whispered. "She's emptying them."

"Maybe they've expired."

"Mom, you know they don't care about that sort of thing here," said Betty. "I think she's stealing stuff."

"Well, run down and tell the manager, dear," said Mordonna. "I'll keep her from leaving."

Mordonna snapped her fingers, and all the wheels on the cart went in different directions. No matter how hard Tracylene tried she could only make it turn in circles. She was about to give up when Betty came back with the manager.

"Not again," he said, grabbing Tracylene by the ear. "Well, that's it. This time I'm calling the police."

He dragged Tracylene off to his office with the girl cursing and swearing revenge on the Floods.

Mordonna got a 90 percent discount on her shopping that night. Tracylene got a fifty-dollar fine and one hundred hours' community service increased to two hundred on account of the name she called the judge.

Community service usually involves the offender's having to go help old people. She or he might have to do their shopping or cut their grass or clean their houses. Tracylene hated old people, and she thought anyone over twenty-five was old. The only people over twenty-five she didn't hate were shortsighted men with even fewer brain cells than she had. She had nine boyfriends like that.

Giving someone like Tracylene community service was like sending a lion who hasn't had any breakfast for a month to help newborn lambs. Every time there was a complaint, she got more hours added to her sentence, and it was impossible for Tracylene to get through more than five minutes without doing something wrong. She was soon headed toward a punishment that would actually take longer than her lifetime even if she lived to ninety.

She lasted at one person's less than an hour.

"Well, yeah, like, it wasn't my fault," she said to her caseworker.

"You put her in the trash can."

"Well, she told me to take out the garbage," said Tracylene. "And have you seen her? She is, like, totally gross and half dead."

Little old ladies with fragile constitutions who normally lived on lettuce and diluted water found their larders packed with baked beans and meat pies after Tracylene had done their shopping for them. They were further distressed by the incredible increase in the cost of everything that meant they had to give her twice as much money as they normally spent.

And so it went. Word got around to the town's old folk, and some of them moved to Florida in case Tracylene was sent to help them. One old lady even went to live in Patagonia. Tracylene's caseworker tried sending her to work at the pig farm, but the pigs got so depressed by her constantly referring to them as bacon that they began to lose weight.

Finally she was sent around the town to pull up the grass that kept growing in the cracks around the edges of the manhole covers. This was the perfect job for her because the grass shriveled up when it saw her coming.

9

Tracylene was the next Dent to go. She was out in the backyard one night, waiting in the bushes for her second-best backup replacement boyfriend. She was wearing her new purple miniskirt with the split up the side and an incredibly bright red lipstick she had bought off the internet that was guaranteed to drive boys wild. On her feet she wore a pair of shoes with such high heels that she had to stand on a box to put them on.

The boy, who had said his name was Jean-Claude but was actually called George, was lost in some bushes at a house across the road. Tracylene was getting so bored waiting that she'd actually started eating her nail polish. As she nibbled at her nails, not realizing they were false and highly toxic, she noticed the hole that Dickie had made in the fence through to number 13.

Maybe Jean-Claude's through there, she thought. *And if he's not, them narkin' Floods got me arrested. Maybe there's something through there I can trash.* She squeezed herself into the Floods' garden. It was quiet, very, very quiet, and dark. The moon was hiding behind the trees, and the only light was from the eerie mushrooms growing on a mound of grass by the clothesline. There were mushrooms that glowed like the luminous numbers on an old clock. Each one, which Betty watered and looked after every single day, was perfect, and Tracylene decided she would rip them out of the ground.

She tottered over to the mound and looked down at it. As she reached down to pull the top off the first mushroom, there was a sucking, popping sound, and a mushroom between her feet vanished into the ground. Tracylene turned to leave, but it was too late. Queen Scratchrot's grave was having its dinner. The grave split open, and a skeleton arm shot out and grabbed Tracylene around the ankle. She fell flat on her face, and before she could make a sound, a second skeleton arm stuffed one of the glowing mushrooms into her mouth and began to drag her into the grave.

While this was going on, Nerlin and Mordonna were sitting side by side on their back veranda, drinking

QUEEN
SCRATCHROT

bloodred Merlinot wine and waiting for the moon to appear. All the children were indoors while their parents relaxed in the cool of the evening.

"Oh, look," said Nerlin. "Your mother's caught something."

"That's nice," said Mordonna. "I wonder what it is. Looks too big to be a cat."

The mushroom spread its glow through Tracylene's entire body until she was shining like a big pink electric dolphin. She whimpered, in the most pathetic voice she could come up with, that she would never be a bad girl again and always get her dad something to drink and even help her mom with whatever it was that mothers do in the kitchen, but because she was lying to try to save herself, no sound came out. This was because if you tell a lie when you are being eaten by a nearly dead queen, you are always struck dumb.

The juice from the mushroom reached right down to the tips of Tracylene's toes and began to tenderize her. Queen Scratchrot had been dead a very long time, and her teeth were not as good as they used to be, so she couldn't eat anything she had to chew.

Tracylene gave one final wobbly pink quiver before the ground opened up and Queen Scratchrot swallowed her. Then there was silence, followed by a very loud belch.

The moon rose high over the Floods' back garden. Nigel and Shirley, Valla's two pet vampire bats, went out to visit all the dogs sleeping outside in the neighboring back-yards.[19] Nerlin and Mordonna rocked gently back and forth on their veranda swing while Queen Scratchrot digested Tracylene with a chorus of burps.

"I'm going indoors," said Nerlin with his hand over his nose. "Something seems to have upset your mother."

"Do you think I should water her grave with some indigestion medicine?" Mordonna asked.

"Good idea, but whatever you do, don't strike a match."

---

[19] *Which just proves that you should always let your dog sleep inside at night. You never know when a hungry vampire bat might be around.*

10

Mrs. Dent didn't put a plate of burger, fries, and beans out for Tracylene each day the way she had for Dickie. She didn't like her daughter and was quite glad she was gone.

"Great useless lump," she said. "She'll be back."

"Who?" asked Mr. Dent. "Tracylene, get me something to drink."

"She's not here," said Mrs. Dent.

"Well, *you* get me one."

But Mrs. Dent wasn't listening. The *Pro-Celebrity See How Many Burgers You Can Eat in Five Minutes While Sitting in a Bath of Beans Championships* had just started, and it was the finals. When Mr. Dent rang the police station, they said he could come and collect his soda, except it had mysteriously evaporated in the bottles and someone had stolen all the bottle tops.

An ad for a range of superhealthy frozen precooked 100 percent taste-free dinners came on, and Mrs. Dent grabbed the phone from her husband.

"Now my daughter's gone missing too," she told Sergeant DaVinci.

There was a silence. The sergeant was one of Tracylene's many boyfriends, and he couldn't decide if he was glad she'd disappeared or if he missed her. Their relationship had always been a bit strange and difficult. For example, one night they'd been to the movies together, and the next day he'd had to arrest her for shoplifting. DaVinci decided that life would be a lot less complicated if he didn't look for Tracylene too efficiently.

"Now, now, Mrs. Dent," he said. "Don't upset yourself. I'm sure she'll turn up."

"I'm not upset," said Mrs. Dent.

"I'll be around shortly," he told her.

"Oh, you needn't bother," said Mrs. Dent. "I don't particularly want you to find her."

"Why did you phone us then?" asked the sergeant, getting suspicious.

"Well, I don't want you to think I did her in. You know, when you find her horribly mangled body somewhere."

"Why do you think she's been horribly mangled?" said the sergeant, getting even more suspicious.

"Well, er, I don't. But when a teenager goes missing on TV, they usually get horribly mangled," said Mrs. Dent, sounding more and more guilty. "She's probably just run off with one of her boyfriends."

"I think you've been watching too much TV," DaVinci said.

"Don't be ridiculous," said Mrs. Dent.

"How can anyone watch *too much* TV?"

The sergeant arrived two minutes later and went over Tracylene's bedroom with a fine-tooth comb. He didn't find any fine teeth, but he did retrieve what he had come for, Tracylene's diary. He read the first few pages, learned two new rude words, and read some stuff that made him feel very strange. He was going to tear out the pages that contained any stuff written about him, but instead he took the diary away to read in bed later with his cocoa.

"When did you last see your daughter?" he asked Mr. and Mrs. Dent.

"Dunno," said Mr. Dent. "Get me something to drink, will you?"

"I'll have some too," said the sergeant.

"Get them yourself. My show's gonna

start," said Mrs. Dent.

The sergeant went back to the station and wrote his report in the special missing persons book. Not the ordinary missing persons book but the special one with the code word on the front: CLASS.[20] Tracylene Dent's details were written on the page after Dickie's.

It didn't take Mr. and Mrs. Dent very long to forget their two children, because that was the sort of people they were. They still shouted and fought a lot and filled their yard with more old cars and trash and threw empty bottles over the fence into all their neighbors' backyards and stole bits off cars, which nearly

---

20 *"Complete Losers and Serial Scumbags," a special police code that meant anyone trying to find any of the people in the book would be arrested.*

got Mr. Dent arrested when he took a fancy to the sirens on police cars and had to make a speedy exit from the station parking lot. Mrs. Dent still stole cigarettes. She just hit other people's children to create a distraction.

Even with half the family gone, the Dents were still the neighbors from hell.

vents decided which Dent would be the next to disappear a few weeks later. Mr. and Mrs. Dent had just had their usual Saturday night fight, the one where Mrs. Dent ended up locked out of the house in the backyard in the rain while Mr. Dent stayed inside with the TV up so loud he couldn't hear her. This was the only way Mr. Dent ever got to watch stuff on TV that *he* wanted.

Mrs. Dent had done her usual beating on the back door and wailing, and now she was doing her falling down in the grass and crying that no one loved her. Quite who she was trying to tell this to was a mystery. Everyone already knew that no one loved her—not even Rambo, the poodle, who, at that very moment, was attempting to kill her left slipper.

Mrs. Dent fell asleep under a bush, with her head poking through the hole in the fence that Dickie and Tracylene had vanished through. Midnight came and went, while Mrs. Dent snored like a pig with a bad sinus problem.

The Floods barely slept. Nighttime was when they did the secret special things that witches and wizards do all over the world. Spells, curses, transforming themselves into huge black bats, drinking blood, and traveling about on broomsticks are just a few of the things that magic people prefer to do under cover of darkness.

Mrs. Dent's snoring interrupted the magic flow. Mordonna's broomstick turned into a dustpan and brush. Valla spilled a glass of his finest blood all over his book of spells, with disastrous results. Nerlin started listening to those dreadful late-night radio shows where sad lonely people phone up, trying to prove to themselves they actually do have lives. Worse still, he actually enjoyed the shows, talked out loud to the radio, and even thought of phoning in himself.

"Is someone trying to saw a tree down out there?" said Mordonna, relieved she had only been a foot in the air when her broomstick had changed.

"No, it's Mrs. Dent snoring," said one of the children.

"Well, it's enough to wake the dead," said Mordonna. "And in our back garden that is not a good thing."

"Oh, no," said Nerlin. "It would be bad enough if your mother woke up, lovely and wonderful though she is, but if it woke Uncle Cloister, there's no knowing what might happen."

"That's not to mention Great-grand-mother Lucreature," said Mordonna. "Winchflat, go out and shut the woman up, there's a good boy."

"Temporarily or permanently?" asked Winchflat.

"Surprise us," said Nerlin.

Winchflat went out into the garden and found Mrs. Dent's head sticking through the fence. She was lying on her back in a patch of stinging nettles with her mouth wide open. Winchflat picked up some dirt and dropped it into Mrs. Dent's mouth.

Mrs. Dent choked, spluttered, and opened her eyes. The skinny, sickly figure of Winchflat towering overhead scared the zombie daylights out of her,[21] and she screamed as loud as someone with a mouthful of dirt can scream. Which is not at all. She rolled onto her front, spit out the dirt, and escaped back into her own yard. The last thing she saw as she wriggled away was something red and shiny. It was half hidden by Winchflat's long, spindly legs, but there was no mistaking what she had seen.

It was one of Tracylene's red high-heeled shoes.

She had a brief flash of nearly being almost but not quite intelligent and said nothing.

Mrs. Dent staggered toward her back door, spitting out dirt and

---

[21] *Zombie daylights are like living daylights, only much more frightening.*

crying. It wasn't knowing her daughter was probably dead that made her so hysterical. Nor was it the terrifying experience she'd just had with Winchflat. No, it was the realization that she'd been asleep for three hours and had missed the final-ever episode of *Mega-Extreme Celebrity Really Dumb Fat Ugly Idiot Loser Makeover*, where they were going to replace someone's entire brain with a silicone implant. She had been looking forward to it all week, and now, quite simply, her life was ruined.

When she woke up at three o'clock the next afternoon, Mrs. Dent remembered the red shoe and reached for the phone.

Sergeant DaVinci was sleeping when the phone rang. Since Dickie and Tracylene had disappeared, Saturday nights had been a lot more relaxed. No one had thrown any bricks through the police station window. And without Tracylene's telling him how much she loved him as she threw up into his police helmet every Friday night, he managed to get a lot more sleep during his weekend shifts. Now that dreadful woman was on the phone again.

"Sergeant," Mrs. Dent cried into the phone, "them weirdos next door killed my daughter, er, er . . ."

"Tracylene," said the sergeant.

"Yeah, her," said Mrs. Dent. "I saw her shoe in their backyard."

"Okay, I'll look into it."

Sergeant DaVinci had never been to the
Floods' house, nor had he ever wanted to.
The place gave him the creeps, but after Mrs.
Dent's call about the shoe, he had no choice. If
there was any actual evidence of foul play,
then Dickie's and Tracylene's disappearances
could no longer be ignored and would have to
be looked into. He would have to rub out their
entries in the CLASS book and rewrite them

in the proper missing persons book, the one that meant he actually had to do something.

He parked his police car down the street outside number 21 and walked back to the Floods' gate. It opened a split second before he touched it and closed as soon as he was through. He turned to open it again, but it growled at him.

"Come in, Forty-two," he said into his walkie-talkie. "Forty-two" was his nickname for his partner, who was waiting in the car. (His real name was Forty-one, Peter Lawrence Henry Forty-one, to be precise.)

"Hello, Sarge," said Forty-two.

"The front gate just growled at me, Forty-two," said the sergeant.

"Sure it did, Sarge."

The sergeant could have sworn he heard

the gate laughing, but he decided not to tell Forty-two about that. He walked up the path to the front door, and a split second before his finger reached it, the bell rang. The door opened, and something small, dark, and very hairy stood there, wagging its back end. It was Satanella.

"What do you want?" asked Satanella.

"Er, um," said the sergeant, looking down the hall to see who was talking to him.

"Down here," said Satanella. "What do you want?"

"Right, yes, okay . . . Is your, er, master or mistress in?" DaVinci asked her, not believing he was actually talking to a dog.

"Wait there," said Satanella, and scampered off down the hall.

"Forty-two, you still there?"

"Yes, Sarge."

"A dog just spoke to me. It actually said proper words and—"

"Well, well, that's nice," said Forty-two into the car radio while he reached for his cell phone. He wondered how long it would take for an ambulance and a doctor with a powerful sedative and a straitjacket to arrive.

"Good afternoon," said Mordonna, appearing from nowhere in the hallway. "What can we do for you?"

The sergeant was captivated. Mordonna had left her sunglasses off, and it's a well-known fact that anyone who looks into her eyes falls hopelessly head over heels in love with her. Nerlin did it several times a day.

"I, um, er, um," Sergeant DaVinci stammered, and followed Mordonna into the kitchen like a devoted puppy.

"Sit down and tell me what the problem is," said Mordonna.

"Well, my boss doesn't understand me. Every time I apply for a promotion he chooses someone else, and now I've started to go bald," the sergeant said.

"No, no. I mean, why are you here?"

"Oh, that is so true. *Why* am I here?" said the sergeant. "Why are any of us here? What does it all *mean*?"

"No, why have you come to my house?" asked Mordonna.

"Shoes," the sergeant replied. "Red shoes."

"These shoes?" said Mordonna, holding up the high heels.

"Tracylene's shoes."

"Yes, that nasty girl." Mordonna's eyes narrowed as she spoke. She put her sunglasses on and released the policeman from her enchanting powers.

"My mother enjoyed her very much," she added.

"Your mother?" said DaVinci.

"Yes, my mother. She's buried in the back garden. Do you want to meet her?"

"Meet her? Buried . . . she's *dead*?"

"Of course she's dead," said Mordonna. "You don't bury people when they're alive, do you?"[22]

"Yeah, but, no, but—excuse me a minute. I have to talk to my partner." Switching on his

---

[22] *Mordonna's uncle Count Septic von Pus had actually been buried alive as a birthday present one year and had liked it so much he had stayed buried for the next fifty years until he died. Then he was dug up and cremated.*

walkie-talkie, the sergeant hurried out into the hall.

"Forty-two, are you there?"

"Er, yes," Forty-two replied cautiously. The ambulance was still ten minutes away, so he had to play for time.

"I need a team of officers with shovels," DaVinci told him.

"Sure you do," said Forty-two slowly.

"I think the girl's buried in the backyard, and I believe they might have buried an old lady there too, while she was still alive," said the sergeant.

"Okay. Excellent. Well done, Sarge," said Forty-two. "There aren't any more talking animals or gates, are there?"

"No, no. Just phone for backup, like I told you," DaVinci ordered.

"No worries, Sarge. I've done that already. They should be here in a few minutes. You just play for time."

"Okay, that's sorted out then," said the sergeant, walking back into the Floods' kitchen. "Any chance of a cup of tea?"

"Tea? Tea? I don't think we've got any tea," Mordonna replied. "Got a nice drop of chilled bat's blood."

"No, no, that's fine. I'll just have a glass of water."

"Okay. Have a nice glass of chilled water from our lovely new fridge," said Mordonna.

"Would you like a frog's eye in it?"

"No, it's all right. I'm not actually that thirsty," said the sergeant. "Maybe we could have a look in the back garden."

"Yes, of course. I was telling Mother about you while you were talking to your partner just now. Follow me."

They walked outside, and there, as Mordonna had said, was a grave, right in the middle of the lawn next to the clothesline.

"This is the policeman I was telling you about, Mother," Mordonna shouted down at the grave. There was silence for a moment. "Oh, all right, Mother."

Turning back to DaVinci, she added, "Sorry I had to shout. Mother's a bit deaf. She wants to shake your hand."

"Of course she does," said the sergeant, and

walked over to the graveside.

The ground opened, and a skinny skeleton arm appeared.

"Mother says just shake her hand. She only lets wizards kiss it."

The sergeant fainted.

When Forty-two, three large ambulance men, and a doctor arrived five minutes later, Sergeant DaVinci was lying on the couch in the Floods' lounge room. He was mumbling to himself and drooling into his walkie-talkie.

"I'm terribly sorry about all this, madam," said the doctor. "It's the strain of the job."

"I understand," said Mordonna from behind her dark glasses.

Satanella made pretend happy little yappy dog noises as one of the ambulance men

tickled her tummy. The doctor gave the
sergeant a powerful sedative, and then they
took him away to the madhouse in a straitjacket.

Sergeant DaVinci spent a very long time
resting and being given large doses of
strange medicine at the Sunshine Home for
the Really Stressed before going off to live
all alone by the sea in a small damp apart-
ment with no water-
front views. Now
and then, over
the following
years, there
were nights when
he would wake up
screaming because
he knew what

144

he had heard and seen had not been in his imagination. He knew without a doubt that the Floods had ruined his brilliant career long before it had reached its peak.

Thoughts of revenge grew dark and evil in his heart. Somehow, somewhere, he would get revenge.

A couple of weeks after the sergeant had been taken away, Mrs. Dent went into Tracylene's old bedroom and remembered that she'd once had a daughter. Mr. Dent had already filled Dickie's room with bits of old motorbike, some buckets of grease, and 1,227 empty cans. But apart from taking Tracylene's parakeet, Adolf, down to the kitchen, where he got fat on a diet of pizza crusts and kept telling Mr. Dent he needed more lipstick, neither parent had been in her room since.

I wonder what happened to Tracylene, Mrs. Dent thought, and then she remembered the red shoes. She had always liked those shoes. After all, they'd been hers until her feet had gotten too fat to fit into them. They were the sort of shoes that made you feel like a princess even if you were really slightly lower than a toad in the evolutionary chain.

She rang the police station, but since the sergeant had been taken away, they had decided on a new policy, and that was to pretend the Dents did not exist. The whole family had just been in the sick sergeant's imagination.

"I'm sorry, madam," they said to Mrs. Dent. "The case is closed."

"But my daughter," said Mrs. Dent, "she's missing."

"Congratulations," said the policeman, and put the phone down.

Mrs. Dent wasn't that bothered—she was more interested in finding out if there was a fattest parakeet in the world category on the *Guinness World Records* TV show—but there were rare moments when she actually missed her children. Moments like when she went to steal cigarettes and there were no small children in the shop for her to hit or when her eyeliner was empty and she wanted to use some of Tracylene's. She couldn't put her finger on a reason, but somewhere in her weird brain was the thought that the Floods had something to do with the disappearance of her children and her lovely red shoes.

"Yeah, them weirdos probably ate them," said Mr. Dent. "Get me something to drink."

"Yeah, narkin' weirdos," said Mrs. Dent, and she actually not only got him a drink but even put ice in it.

That night, when most of the world was asleep, Mrs. Dent forced herself through the hole in the fence into the Floods' back garden. Tracylene might be missing, but at least Mrs. Dent knew where her shoes were. And those weirdos weren't going to get to keep them; she'd get them back if it was the last thing she did. She hadn't eaten any fries since breakfast, so there was a good chance she might have lost enough weight to get her feet into the shoes again.

It was as quiet as the grave, which wasn't really surprising considering how many people were buried there. Incredibly, one of Tracylene's red shoes was there by the queen's grave. Mrs. Dent took off her slipper and put it on.[23] She would have thought about the story of Cinderella, except "Cinderella" was much too big a word to fit inside her head. Now she had to find the other shoe. She eyed the Floods' back door and started forward.

Upstairs in one of the back bedrooms, Winchflat, the family's computer genius, was doing what he did most nights, following strange people around the world on the internet. As midnight fell in one chatroom, he moved on to the next time zone. On the net Winchflat was a legend. He could hack into anything and

---

[23] *She didn't so much put the shoe on as jam three of her toes into it and then find she was unable to get them out again.*

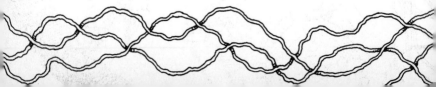

had once made the whole of America bankrupt in a single night, just for the fun of it. When he put all the money back the next day, he made all the poor people a bit richer and all the rich people quite a bit poorer. Of course it was all

hushed up, but all the superhackers knew Winchflat (or Naughty Trixie, as he was known on the net) had been there.

The night Mrs. Dent came into their back garden, Winchflat was standing by the window drinking a can of Super-High-Caffeine-Zap-a-Cola when he looked down and saw her stumbling about on the lawn in a single red high heel. He immediately went and told the others.

"The hippo has landed. And she's heading this way."

"What should we do?" said Mordonna.

"What does the wretched woman do that annoys us the most?" asked Nerlin.

"Breathe?" said Winchflat.

"The thing that affects everyone the most is her TV blaring out all day and night. That's it!

Let's turn *her* into a television!" Mordonna said.

"Brilliant," said Nerlin.

"Are we all agreed?" said Mordonna.

They were.

"Right, we'll draw straws," Nerlin said when no one volunteered. "Everyone get a pencil and paper, and whoever draws the longest straw will do the magic."

You might be wondering why Nerlin didn't just do the magic himself. Well, I'm going to let you in on a very secret secret that no one who isn't a wizard or witch knows. It will also explain why Nerlin took Merlinmary with him when he went to talk to Mr. Dent and why it was Merlinmary who turned Rambo into a poodle. Before I do, you must promise inside your head that you will never tell this secret to anyone else.

If you look at all the stories about wizards, from Merlin through to Harry Potter, you will see that not many of them get married and have children. You might think this is because most wizards are seriously ugly, but that's not the case. Most witches actually think wizards look really cool and handsome. No, the reason is this: When a wizard is born, he has magical powers, but if he has a child, that child takes some of his father's magical powers. And as the child grows, so do his magical powers, but the bit his father gave him is not replaced. This means that Nerlin, who has had seven children, has lost a lot of his magic.

It doesn't matter how the children are made—in a laboratory, grown from a cutting, or made the way you and I were—the wizard always loses a bit of his power.

Now the only thing that Nerlin can turn a person into is a potted plant. He has even lost the power to make someone become a frog or a toad.

When people call him Merlin, as they do all the time, he explains that N comes after M, and he came after Merlin, so that was why he was called Nerlin. Sensible people look

confused at this and just nod. Foolish people look sarcastic and ask him why his sons aren't called Oerlin, Perlin, and Qerlin then. These people usually get turned into geraniums.

"Couldn't you try to turn them into useful herbs, like parsley and mint and deadly nightshade?" Mordonna would ask. "I hate geraniums, with all their horrible bright, happy flowers."

The Floods are a very close, loving family, so they make sure that no outsiders ever discover Nerlin's secret. They're not likely to anyway. Nerlin is very tall, wears a big black cloak, and looks seriously evil. Only complete idiots ever say, "You haven't got any magical power," and they're better off as potted plants anyway.

Nerlin's loss of powers do make him quite depressed, though. "I've lost my magic," he says to Mordonna when they're alone. "How can you love a man with no magic?"

"You'll always be magic to me, my darling," Mordonna tells him. "Have you thought of potted chrysanthemums? They're much nicer than geraniums, and they're the flower of death, too."

"I don't choose geraniums deliberately, my angel," Nerlin says. "I try to make other plants, but they always turn out geraniums. I hate geraniums."

The obvious solution would have been for Mordonna to turn them into other plants herself. She could have done it

easily, but she never did. It would have
made Nerlin even more depressed.

Betty drew the longest and most artistic-looking straw, so she was the one who would do the magic. She opened the back door.

"Hello, Mrs. Dent," she said.

Mrs. Dent tripped over her heel and fell flat on her face. Queen Scratchrot's arms poked out of her grave and started waving around.

"Drop it!" shouted Betty before her granny could get a grip. "Are you looking for something?"

"You stole my shoes, didn't you?" said Mrs. Dent, struggling to her feet. She started to limp toward the house. "I'll get youse!"

"Yes, you will," said Betty. "You'll get us

lots of lovely wildlife documentaries and fancy films with subtitles."

"And *no* reality shows at all," said Winchflat.

Mordonna put her arm around Betty and said, "Look, darling, I know you drew the best straw, but maybe you better let someone else do the magic. You know how your tricks sometimes don't work out quite how you plan them, and we don't want her turned into a cabin cruiser or a hot-air balloon."

Mrs. Dent hobbled across the veranda and lunged for the door. As she tripped and fell inside, Winchflat snapped his fingers. There was a quick flash, and a split second later she turned into a television—and not an ordinary plasma one, either, but the very best and most expensive television money could buy, a Super

High-Definition, Backlit, Sidelit, AND Frontlit LCD Television with Fifteen-Channel Surround Sound and an Air-Conditioned Voice Command Remote Control.

It was poetic really. Mrs. Dent became the one thing she had wanted to own more than anything in the whole world.

Mr. Dent didn't notice his wife had gone until the following night.

Something wasn't right. He could sense it, but he couldn't put his finger on it. It was only a subtle change, and Mr. Dent didn't do subtle. Then it dawned on him. It was the smell.

As always, every single square inch of the house smelled of burgers, fries, and beans. But that night something was missing.

Instead of a new cloud of hot, greasy mist hovering in the air, there was just the old, cold smell like first thing in the morning. Except now it was the evening.

"Oi," he shouted.

"Oi" was what Mr. and Mrs. Dent called each other when they weren't fighting.

"Oi, where's me dinner? Gimme something to drink."

Silence.

"I said, where's me narkin' dinner?" Mr. Dent shouted.

More silence, interrupted by the sound of Rambo scratching at the back door. Mr. Dent fell asleep again, but ten minutes later the dog's barking woke him up, and he did something he hadn't done for years. He went into the kitchen.

"What's all this stuff?" he said, looking at

the kettle and the stove and the toaster.

Mrs. Dent wasn't there. Nor was she in the bedroom, the bathroom, or the backyard. Mr. Dent didn't look in the garage or his shed because women were not allowed in there. The more he didn't find Mrs. Dent, the more angry he became.

Even the back door was against him, so he kicked it in, before he remembered he was not wearing his strong boots. Mr. Dent staggered back to his chair and fell asleep again while *Pro-Celebrity Wife Swap USA* started. This made him even more bad-tempered because it was his favorite show. He would often daydream about swapping Mrs. Dent for a big red sports car and then fall asleep and have a nightmare where he'd swapped her for her mother.

It was dark when he woke up, and his stomach was calling out for burger, fries, and beans.

"Oi, where's my dinner? Get me something to drink," he shouted.

Silence.

But he was not alone. There was a tall figure silhouetted in the glow from the television. She snapped her fingers, and the TV fell silent.

"Hello, Mr. Dent," said Mordonna. "Mrs. Dent isn't here. Why don't you come and have dinner at our house?"

Mordonna had not gone to the Dents' house with any evil plans in her head. The Floods are basically a kind, loving family who are always willing to give people a second chance, or in Mr. Dent's case, a fifty-third chance. Realizing that he was now on his own, Mordonna had decided she would try to turn him into as normal a human being as possible.

"If it works," she said to her family, who thought she was probably wasting her time, "we can always get Winchflat to make him a nice new wife out of some spiders and a goat."

"Your trouble, my darling," said Nerlin, "is that you are just too nice. Trying to save Mr. Dent is like trying to push half a peanut up Mount Everest with a salmon's feather."

"Um, I think you'll find salmon don't have

feathers," said Betty.

"My point exactly," said Nerlin.

"Well it's worth a try," said Mordonna, though as she stood in Mr. Dent's living room, she knew in her heart, she had no chance.

"Gimme a drink . . ." Mr. Dent began.

Then he realized who he was talking to. He tried to get up, but there was a terrible pain in his right foot. Rambo, who hadn't had any dinner either, was chewing on his big toe. Mr. Dent started to swear, but Mordonna took off her dark glasses, which should have hypnotized him. Her eyes glowed like fire, but Mr. Dent was too mad for them to have their full effect. His foot hurt. His ankle hurt. He was beginning to suffer saturated fat and cholesterol withdrawal, and now this witch was trying to hypnotize him.

"Gimme . . ." he spluttered, struggling up from his chair.

He tripped over Rambo and onto the coffee table, which collapsed. At this point someone with a few more brain cells than the fourteen Mr. Dent had would have gone very quiet and still.

Mr. Dent opened his mouth and demonstrated to Mordonna what an enormous vocabulary of rude words he had.

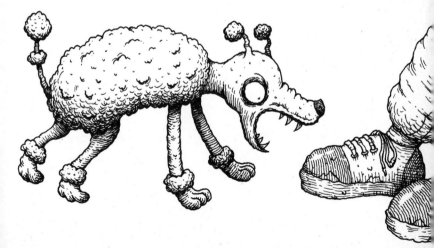

"Naughty, naughty," said Mordonna. "Don't you know there are children present?" She gestured to Betty, who had been standing behind her.

Lots more swearwords, some of which Mordonna had to pretend to Betty meant far nicer things than they actually did.

"Haven't you ever done any housework?" asked Mordonna, looking around at the mess.

"Well, it's time to start," said Betty. "This place is a pigsty, without the intelligent pigs."

Mr. Dent charged toward them on all fours, pain in his foot and murder in his heart.

"Mr. Dent is like a little piggy, isn't he, Betty?" said Mordonna. "It's sad to see anyone living this way."

"Yes, Mother. He should be a cleaner—"

Betty had intended to say, "He should be a

cleaner piggy," but as soon as she said the word "cleaner," there was a flash of light that cut off her words.

The pain in Mr. Dent's right foot vanished. It happened so suddenly he sat up and looked at his feet. Then he fainted.

Mr. Dent's feet weren't feet anymore. They were wheels, small, round, shiny wheels. Mr. Dent felt himself shrinking and changing shape. His skin was changing too. Now it wasn't what you'd call skin; it was what you'd call stainless steel.

"Oops," said Betty. "Sorry, Mother. Think I got it wrong again."

"Don't apologize, darling," said Mordonna. "The stainless steel matches the fridge and the TV. I can see a family resemblance."

A few seconds later the transformation was

complete. What had once been a lazy pig of a man was now the best vacuum cleaner in the world. Mr. Dent was the ultimate vacuum cleaner. He was a cordless automatic robot vacuum cleaner that could back his bottom up to an electric socket and plug himself in whenever his batteries started going flat. While everyone was resting or out, Mr. Dent went quietly and efficiently around the whole house, stairs included, sucking up dust. He even had an extralong nozzle that got cobwebs off the ceiling and a special attachment for getting Satanella's and Merlinmary's hair off the furniture. And when his bag was full, Mr. Dent went out into the garden and emptied himself into the trash before starting the whole thing all over again.

Now, in a normal house, getting all the dusting and cleaning done automatically would be great. But it wasn't like that in the Floods' house. The Floods had cobwebs that were old friends. Generations of spiders had lived in complete safety on the ceilings and windows, knowing that no one was ever going to come and sweep them away. They had dust collected in happy piles around the house that just moved to one side when anyone needed to go past.

With magic that was meant to happen, it was always possible to change your mind, but because Betty's magic was so uncontrolled, no one knew the formula, which made changing it pretty dangerous. If they made a mistake, Mr. Dent could turn into something covered in mold that smelled like a bad drain and kept exploding. On the other hand, he could change into something awful.

So once again Winchflat sorted things out. He took the Dent-O-Vac down to his special workshop in the cellars and made a few modifications. Basically, he made Mr. Dent run backward (which anyone who had known him as a human would have said he'd done all his life). Every morning Mr. Dent trundled out into the garden and collected dust and flies. Then he spent the rest of the day spreading the dust around the house and feeding the flies to the spiders. At midnight, when his work was done, he would trundle into the kitchen and sit next to Dickie, the fridge, and

the two of them would hum softly together in a very loving father-and-son-bonding way, as they had never done when they were human.

Once the final Dent was gone, Rambo's bad temper vanished, and he became a cuddly, fluffy, happy little poodle. He went to live with the nice neighbors at number 15, an old couple who spoiled him rotten with poached chicken, crispy liver treats, and a red velvet cushion to sleep on.

Mordonna turned the Dents' other pet, Adolf, the parakeet, into a bluebird. The Floods even found him a bluebird wife, and the two of them built a nest in a tree in the Floods' backyard so Adolf could always be close to Tracylene, who he'd quite liked except when she had painted his claws and beak with red nail varnish.

When you are as dreadful as the Dents were, all your relatives pretend they don't know you. Sometimes they move to another town, and sometimes they even move to Patagonia. No one knew if the Dents had any relatives, but if they had, they were never found.[24] There was a rumor that rather than

---

[24] *If you had relatives like the Dents, would you want to admit it?*

have anyone know they were related to them, their cousins had gone to live in a remote shack high up in the Andes. So no one missed the Dents. There was even talk of a big block party to celebrate.

If a family of nice people disappeared, the place would be crawling with detectives with big flashlights looking for clues. They would fingerprint every square inch of the house. They would scrape DNA out of the bottom of the garbage cans, trying to find out what had happened. No stone would be left unturned.

But when all the Dents vanished, the police raced into action by buying the biggest bottle of champagne they could find and celebrating for three days. They put the news in their monthly newsletter, in the "Good News" section, and everyone kept his fingers crossed just to make sure the Dents wouldn't come back.

After a couple of months the bank, which owned nearly all of the Dents' house, put up a For Sale sign. The house would be auctioned off in a week's time.

"I hope the next owners are all right," said Betty.

"Mmm," said Nerlin.

"What?" said Mordonna. "Have you got a plan?"

"Well," said Nerlin, "there is a way to make *sure* we like the new owners."

"How?"

"We become the new owners," said Nerlin.

"You mean, move next door?" asked Betty. "But who will live here?"

"We will," said Nerlin. "Look, there're nine of us, not to mention the corpses and ghosts. We could do with more room."

So that's what they did.

If you went to an auction and saw a family that looked like the Floods standing there, you'd have to be pretty brave to bid against them. And if you saw how spooky and weird the Floods' house and garden were next door, you probably wouldn't want to live there anyway. Because of this, there were very few people at the auction outside number 11 Acacia Avenue. There was the standard property developer, who wanted to pull the house down and build apartments, and there were five people who had seen all the junk in the front yard and thought it was a garage sale.

Mordonna went up to the property developer and whispered in his ear. He walked off in silence.

"What did you say to him?" asked Nerlin.

"I asked him if he had ever thought what life would be like if he had sticky feet and could cling to glass," said Mordonna.

The auctioneer climbed up on a box and held up his hand. "Who will start the bidding?" he said.

"Two hundred and fifty—" the property developer started to say, but before he could finish, there was a gentle plop, and the property developer decided that he'd rather spend the rest of his life

eating flies and hopped off into the grass.

Then there was silence.

"Come on," said the auctioneer. "Who will give me three hundred thousand?"

"Twelve dollars," Betty called out.

"Twelve dollars? *Twelve* dollars?" said the auctioneer. "Come on, people. This house has to be sold today."

"I'll give you four dollars for the old washing machine," said one of the five bargain hunters.

"I've changed my mind," said Betty. "Ten dollars."

More nervous silence.

The auctioneer would have cried, except people who sell houses can't cry, because the bits of their brains that have feelings have been removed.

"Two hundred thousand, please?"

Silence, followed by everyone except the Floods walking nervously away.

"One hundred thousand . . . please?"

A very long silence.

"Who bid ten dollars?" the auctioneer asked.

"I did," said Betty.

"You're too young."

"Ten dollars and five cents," said Betty. "And if you check part three, subsection eighteen, page seven hundred thirty-five of volume forty-seven of the houseowning code, I think you'll find that anyone over the age of two is allowed to buy a house."

This of course was completely made up, but the auctioneer didn't know that. Anyway, he realized that ten dollars and five cents was better than no dollars and the disgrace of being the first auctioneer ever in the whole town not to sell a house at auction.

"Okay, okay, any advance on ten dollars and five cents?" he asked.

The auctioneer waited for fifteen minutes, shuffling his feet and trying not to cry onto his clipboard. In spite of all his years of training at auctioneer school, he knew no one was going to make a better offer. He knew he was now in Auctioneer Nightmare Land, not that terrible place that creeps into every salesperson's nightmares where he actually sells something for what it is really worth, but that terrible, terrible place of dark terror where he actually sells something for a lot less than it is really worth. He even thought of buying the house himself just to save his professional pride, but he was already the proud owner of seven really massive mortgages. Finally he couldn't delay it any longer. He lifted his shaking hand and said, "Ten dollars and five cents, going once, going twice, going three times . . . gone."

Betty gave him ten dollars and ten cents and said he could keep the change, and the Floods promised they would never tell anyone how much they had paid for the house.

The Floods got back the ten dollars and ten cents by selling all the rubbish in the Dents' front yard to the garage-sale man for twenty-five dollars. The garage-sale man came with a big truck and took away all the old cars, washing machines, fridges, bottles, and other junk. He thought he'd gotten the bargain of the century. The Floods *had* gotten the bargain of the century, and after the impromptu garage sale they now had a tidy front yard and enough money left over for each of them to buy a lottery ticket that, because they could do magic, won them just enough money to make sure they never had to worry about the bills.

School vacation began, and the whole Flood family spent the next two weeks having a backyard and indoors blitz until the ex-Dent house was perfect. It took some very powerful magic to shift all the layers of burger grease that covered everything. It was impossible to make it vanish completely. The best they could do was gather it all up in one big ball of fat and send it across the other side of the world to a small tropical island where people still talk of the day the giant asteroid of lard from the heavens landed on their beach. They see it as proof that they are the Chosen People.

"Now that we've got all this extra space," Mordonna said, "maybe I should have another baby."

"Er, um, I'm just going down to my shed," said Nerlin. He had taken over Mr. Dent's shed and was discovering all the wonderful things that guys did in their sheds, like sit around in dirty old armchairs listening to broken radios while they rubbed oil into lots and lots of wrenches and chisels that they would never use for anything.

The twins pulled down the fence between the two backyards, giving the family enough room to bury several more dead relatives who had come with them from Transylvania Waters and had been stored in old jam jars in one of the deepest cellars with only the night eels for company.

"Great idea," said Mordonna. "Mother's been complaining that she's got no one to talk to apart from the worms, and now that they've eaten the last bits of skin, even they don't visit her anymore."

They decided to bring in one dead relative from each side of the family, Great-Aunt Blodwen and Uncle Flatulence. When they had settled in, they'd bury a couple more.

"I've got a soft spot for Great-Aunt Blodwen," said Nerlin. "It's over there by the new veggie garden."

Winchflat built another one of his brilliant machines, the iCellar, Dungeon, and Moat[25] Replicator, which photocopied all the tunnels

---

[25] *Because the Floods don't live in a castle, they keep their moat in thousands of bottles in the wine cellar.*

and cellars under the Floods' house, turned them back to front, and moved them under the Dents' old house, then joined up the two sets. Merlinmary connected everything to her lead-lined bed and even strung some tiny black lights around Nerlin's shed.

They decided to keep both kitchens because they all agreed they would be much happier if Satanella had somewhere to eat where the

others didn't have to watch, smell, or hear her.

As the school vacation came to an end, Valla gave the windows their final coat of dust and black paint, Betty planted the last patch of poison ivy in the flower beds, and the other children spent two frantic days doing all the wizard school homework they should have done two weeks before.

The last day of vacation was, like everywhere, weird. It was still vacation, so you could do what you liked, but whatever you did never seemed that great because you knew tomorrow you'd be back at school.

The whole family sat on the back veranda as the ice-cold moon rose over the trees and cast its peaceful light over the two fresh graves.

"Listen to that," said Mordonna.

"What? I can't hear anything," said Nerlin.

"Exactly."

Life, at last, was perfect.[26]

----

26 *Apart from Satanella's trying to dig up Uncle Flatulence.*

The
Flood Family
Files

Nerlin

Nerlin is the great-great-grandson of Merlin, the most famous wizard who ever lived. Despite what he tells people, he would have been called Merlin, but at his Deviling (like a Christening for wizards) the priest had a terrible cold.

LIKES: Square tables

DISLIKES: Round tables and people called Arthur, and drains

HOBBIES: Stamp collecting

PETS: None of his own, but takes care of everyone else's

FAVORITE COLOR: Transparent

FAVORITE FOOD: Banquets

Mordonna

In the world of witchcraft and magic, Mordonna is a legend. Magicians and wizards fall at her feet just to smell the dirt between her toes. Yet for all her staggering beauty and mystery, she is an unspoiled down-to-earth housewife who likes nothing more than a quiet evening at home with her family, sucking the insides out of lizards and watching *Susan the Teenage Human* on TV.

LIKES: Her family

DISLIKES: Cats and cardigans

HOBBIES: Knitting cardigans ~~for~~ from cats

PETS: Nerlin and a senile vulture called Leach

FAVORITE COLOR: Red

FAVORITE FOOD: Diet blood

(Leach flew in through the window the day Mordonna was born and has been her devoted slave ever since. Now that he is so old, someone else has to prechew his carrion for him. You don't want to know who that is, but the name rhymes with Jack Donalds.)

Valla, 22

Valla is the eldest of the Flood children. He is the only one in the family to have a proper job. He works as the manager of the local blood bank and often brings his work home with him.

LIKES: Blood

DISLIKES: Anything that isn't blood

HOBBIES: Looking at blood through a very big microscope

PETS: Nigel and Shirley, his two vampire bats[27]

FAVORITE COLOR: Red

FAVORITE FOOD: Hot blood

---

[27] *Nigel and Shirley won gold for Belgium in the 1984 World Ice Dance Championships.*

Satanella, 16

Satanella was once a little girl as pretty as a bag of eels, but after a terrible accident with a shrimp and a faulty wand, she was turned into a small dog.

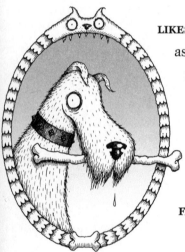

LIKES: Anything that can't run as fast as she can

DISLIKES: Anything that can run faster than she can

HOBBIES: Biting things

PETS: A squeaky rubber human called Alan[28]

FAVORITE COLOR: Blurry fast-moving skin color

---

[28] *Alan was originally a drains inspector who examined the Floods' drain a bit too closely. He is much happier now.*

Merlinmary, 15

No one is sure if Merlinmary is a boy or a girl. Even Merlinmary doesn't know. Merlinmary's greatest talent is making electricity, which he/she does all the time.

LIKES: Thunderstorms with lots of lightning

DISLIKES: Gas

HOBBIES: Putting light-bulbs in his/her ears and making them light up

PETS: Several cockroaches[29]

FAVORITE COLOR: Violent yellow

FAVORITE FOOD: Fuse wire

---

[29] *Including Henri, a cockroach from Paris who once won a stage in the Tour de France.*

Winchflat, 14

Although he looks as if he has been dead for a long time, Winchflat is the family genius. He can outwit the fastest computer and count to eleven on his fingers (seventeen if he uses his toes too).

LIKES: Nerds, especially undead zombie nerds

DISLIKES: Daylight

HOBBIES: Chatrooms, or even better: chat-dungeons

PETS: A very big dictionary called Trevor

FAVORITE COLOR: Darkness

FAVORITE FOOD: Caffeine

Morbid and Silent, 11

Morbid and Silent are twins. To the untrained eye they are identical twins, but actually they are mirror twins, which means they are identical in every way except horizontally. They are like the reflection of each other in the mirror. Morbid is right-handed; Silent is left-handed—except during the full moon, when they change places. They communicate with each other by telepathy.

LIKES: Silence

DISLIKES: Not silence

HOBBIES: Being silent

PETS: Each other

FAVORITE COLOR: Each other

FAVORITE FOOD: Anything that doesn't make a noise when you eat it (except anything that ends with "mite," of course)

Betty, 10

After having six strange children, Mordonna decided she wanted a normal pretty little girl she could cook and sew with. So she had Betty, who looks like a china doll. Unlike the rest of the children, who go to a special school in Patagonia, Betty goes to the ordinary school just down the road. She may look normal, but she still has awesome powers.

LIKES: Everything

DISLIKES: Nothing

HOBBIES: Embroidery, pressing flowers, washing dishes

PETS: A scraggy black cat called Vlad

FAVORITE COLOR: Pink

FAVORITE FOOD: Cotton candy (leech flavor)

Family Pets

DORIS THE DODO

Everyone knows that dodos are extinct. Humans discovered them in 1598 and in less than a hundred years managed to kill every single one. All except Doris, who is now 350 years old, although for 345 years of that time she was an egg, until Winchflat built his incredible iDodo Egg Hatching Machine.

Unfortunately they haven't managed to find another egg, so Winchflat is now building an iDodo Hydrostatic Dodo Cloning Photocopier. One day we may see huge colonies of dodos roaming free, falling out of trees, and walking into things.[30]

---

[30] *Dodos can't fly, and their eyesight is terrible, so it's not surprising they got wiped out.*

THE NIGHT EELS

Night eels live in total darkness, and if even the slightest pinprick of light appears—like the faint neon light that tells you the battery on your cell phone is nearly dead—they explode. You only know they exist when you feel them, soft and wet and slippery, as they slide over your skin like wet velvet. If they like you, they wrap themselves around your face and stick their heads up one of your nostrils and

their tails up the other. If you have three nostrils, they bring a friend. If they don't like you, they do the same thing but with electricity and more slime. Winchflat tried to teach some night eels to sing, but the only noise they made was so depressing he couldn't bear to be with them for more than a few minutes a day.

How to Build a Massive-Electric-Shock Dead-Person-iReviver

YOU WILL NEED:

1 dead person to revive
10 dead people to practice on
1 Krankovich 476B Portable Nuclear Reactor

17 feet of big copper wire with bright red
insulation

1 colossal power source, e.g., the sun or
Merlinmary

Strong glue—sometimes the skull can burst
open

Heavy-duty rubber gloves and boots

Goggles, in case of flying toes

Blood spurting out of the dead person's nose is an unavoidable side effect. Some people think this is a bonus.

The dead person's pajamas nearly always catch fire. (Good thing too.)

the FLOODS
SCHOOL PLOT

COLIN THOMPSON
ILLUSTRATED BY CRAB SCRAMBLY

Coming Next

In the next book about the Floods: everything you ever wanted to know about wizard school, and lots of stuff you never even thought of. Quicklime College is a proper wizard and witch school far away in the deepest mountains of Patagonia. They don't waste their time playing baby games on broomsticks there. They learn useful, important things, like how to turn people into slugs and how to steal valuable jewels and gold from impenetrable castles.[31]

THINGS YOU WON'T LEARN AT QUICKLIME:

Smiling
How to make tea
How to kick a ball around in a field of mud
    with twenty-one other people

---

[31] *And how to make a magic potion (using only spit, evaporated water, and a fish eye) that makes everyone think you are so wonderful, they want to give you anything you want.*

How to juggle three tennis balls
Welsh
Beige

THINGS YOU WILL LEARN AT QUICKLIME:

Scowling
How to make warts
How to kick a massive lump of dinosaur gristle
    around in a field of mud with thirteen other
    people
How to juggle three tennis players
Seriously powerful magic[32]
Time travel
Time travel

---

[32] *Including Invisiblits for Year 8 and over.*

About the Author

COLIN THOMPSON was born in England but finally had the good sense to move to Australia in 1995.

As you can see from the picture below, it took him a *really* long time to write this book.

BORN: Yes

DISLIKES: Windows

BEST THING THAT IS SMALL AND BLACK AND SHINY: My PSP

PETS: Dogs: Bonnie, Max, and Charlie

FAVORITE COLOR: Silly question. I like blue for jeans, but I wouldn't want to eat blue food (unless it was cake)

FAVORITE FOOD: Cherries

BEST PICTURE BOOK I'VE DONE: *How to Live Forever*

BEST NOVEL I'VE WRITTEN: *How to Live Forever*

Okay, that's enough. I'm off to cut the grass.